Samuel French Acting Edition

I0591797

Scrambled Feet

Book, Music & Lyrics by
John Driver and Jeffrey Haddow

SAMUELFRENCH.COM   SAMUELFRENCH.CO.UK

FOR PRODUCTION ENQUIRIES

UNITED STATES AND CANADA
Info@SamuelFrench.com
1-866-598-8449

UNITED KINGDOM AND EUROPE
Plays@SamuelFrench.co.uk
020-7255-4302

Each title is subject to availability from Samuel French, depending upon country of performance. Please be aware that *SCRAMBLED FEET* may not be licensed by Samuel French in your territory. Professional and amateur producers should contact the nearest Samuel French office or licensing partner to verify availability.

THE CAST

SCRAMBLED FEET, by John Driver and Jeffrey Haddow, musical direction and arrangements by Jimmy Wisner and Roger Neil. Settings by Ernest Allen Smith; costumes by Kenneth M. Yount; lighting by Robert F. Strohmeier; assistant musical director and additional arrangements by Roger Neil. Directed by Mr. Driver, production stage manager, Sari E. Weisman. Presented by John Adams Vaccaro and Jimmy Wisner, in association with Ciro A. Gamboni at the Village Gate, 160 Bleeker Street. With Evalyn Baron, John Driver, Jeffrey Haddow, Roger Neil and Hermione

ACT ONE

Haven't We Met . . .
The Avant Garde Playwrighting Kit
Latin American Tour/Making the Rounds
Agent
Composer/Hungup Tango
Huns/British
Intermission/Could Have Been
Christ & Pontius Pilate
Theatrical Olympics
Theatre Party Ladies

ACT TWO

Warmup Guru
Critic Party Doll
Love in the Wings
Stanislaw/Only One Dance
No Small Roles
Child Star
Sham Dancing
Elizabethan Dinner Theatre
Have You Ever Been On Stage . . .
Advice to Producers
One Happy Family

AUTHORS' NOTE

The names of shows and celebrities used herein are indicative of the New York theatre scene the summer of 1979. These, along with the names of theatres and cities, should be changed and updated to reflect the location and time of your production. For instance, "The Avant-Garde Playwrighting Kit" may be adapted and localized to rake your favorite tin gods over the coals. The main thing is to have fun with it. If you let our show be a stimulating challenge to your creative ingenuity, your cast and audience will have a rare and delightful theatrical experience. Break a leg!

DIRECTOR'S NOTE

This script reflects the roles played by the original New York cast. The various parts may be distributed to different actors in a four person cast (three men, one woman) according to the individual actor's strengths.

Scrambled Feet

HAVEN'T WE MET

(*ROGER at piano. Each performer enters on solo line.*)

ROGER.
HAVEN'T WE MET SOMEWHERE BEFORE?
JEFF.
DID YOU SEE US PLAY BRECHT IN BERLIN
(*enter from 3*)
EVVIE.
OR WAS IT IN FRANCE AT A PLAY BY MOLIERE
(*enter from 2*)
JOHN.
OR WERE YOU OUT FRONT AT THE FOLLIES BERGERE
(*enter from 1*)
ALL.
WHERE HAVE WE SEEN YOUR FACES BEFORE
WAS IT A VAUDEVILLE IN MAINE
JEFF. (BRRRR)
ROGER and EVVIE. (CHILLY)
JOHN. (COLD)
ALL.
WASN'T IT GREECE IN 400 B.C.
ALL OF YOU LOOK SO FAMILIAR TO ME
ALL.
HELLO, CHARLIE, ROBERT, ALICE, HOW HAVE YOU
BEEN?
(*cross D. to apron*)
WHEREVER WE MET WE'RE TOGETHER AGAIN
WITH COMEDY, INSANITY AND SOMETHING MORE
A TOTALLY ORIGINAL MUSICAL SCORE
ALL.
HOW WAS THE SHOW YOU SAW US IN LAST?
(*cross U. to piano*)
WAS IT A HIT OR A FLOP
(GOBBLE, GOBBLE, GOBBLE)

WAS IT CATHARTIC OR DID IT JUST TRY
WERE THE JOKES FUNNY OR DID THEY JUST DIE
(*sit at piano*)
HA, HA, HA, HA, HA, HA, HA, HA, HA, HA, HA, HA,
(*All die.*)
   EVVIE.
HAVEN'T WE SHARED SOME MAGICAL TIMES
   JEFF.
AT STRATFORD ON AVON,
   JEFF and EVVIE.
THE GLOBE
   JOHN.
REMEMBER THOSE NIGHTS AT THE MOSCOW ART
   ALL.
THE CURTAIN MAY FALL BUT WE'RE NEVER APART
(*music competition*)
HELLO, HOW ARE YOU, HOW'VE YOU BEEN
WHEREVER WE MET WE'RE TOGETHER AGAIN
WITH COMEDY, INSANITY AND SOMETHING MORE
A TOTALLY ORIGINAL
GIVE MY REGARDS TO BROADWAY
A TOTALLY ORIGINAL, TOTALLY ORIGINAL,
   TOTALLY ORIGINAL
MUSICAL SCORE!

(*BLACKOUT*)

AVANT GARDE PLAYWRIGHTING KIT

(*EVVIE as "wife" dusting* L., *ROGER as "playwright" enters* 2
  waving check.)

ROGER. Honey! No more peanut butter sandwiches. Hole in
the Wall Theatre is going to produce my play.
EVVIE. Roger, is that you?
JOHN. (*enters 1 as "announcer"*) Just three weeks ago, this
mediocre young playwright was selling hot orlon stocking caps
outside the bus station, and today his option has been picked up.
If you've been rejected by every major producer in the country,
don't be discouraged. The Avant Garde Playwrighting Kit is the
answer to your problem. (*EVVIE & ROGER show kit.*) The
Avant Garde Playwrighting Kit! Everything you need to create

your image as an avant garde playwright; a gypsy headband. (*EVVIE & ROGER show headband.*) An ounce of the finest Bolivian Cocaine. (*EVVIE & ROGER show Cocaine.*) I'll take that. Dark glasses to hide your drug-dilated pupils. (*ROGER shows glasses.*) Drug-dilated Pupils. (*EVVIE shows pupils.*) And to give your apartment the perfect ambience, a box of cockroaches, (*EVVIE shows box.*), and your very own rat. (*ROGER shows rat.*) Yes, we'll let you take your pick from the Avant Garde stable of stock protagonists. Unusual and provocative characters like the Bolshevik dwarf, the disembodied head, and who can forget the old standby, the blind war veteran. (*JEFF enters 2 as "blind veteran, singing "Over There".*) We'll even help you build phony mystique and bogus charisma in your dialogue with rock 'em sock 'em phrases guaranteed to amaze your friends and fool the critics. Hardhitting, realistic lines like:

JEFF. Where the fuck is the chair? (*looking for chair with outstretched arms; finally kicking it, then sitting down in chair R.*)

JOHN. And there's more. You'll learn the theatrical catch-22 casting procedure. (*EVVIE & ROGER cross D.C.*)

EVVIE. Have you worked for us before?

ROGER. No.

EVVIE. I'm sorry. We only use people who have worked for us before.

ROGER. How does anyone get to work for you in the first place?

EVVIE. You have to be born in the building.

JOHN. And from New York, you'll learn the secret Broadway theatre handshake. (*EVVIE kisses ROGER's ass.*) And, if you act now, at no extra cost, we'll send you this rare nostalgic recording of Samuel Beckett's greatest hits. You'll hear such Classics as (*Cast makes funny sounds.*) or this hummable tune, and from the San Francisco Mime Troupe (*Cast does nothing*). Yes, a truly amazing record! And for the first two hundred aspiring playwrights who apply you will receive as an extraadded bonus, this complete set of writing implements.

ROGER. (*holding up shovel and making digging motions*) It really works.

JOHN. Worried about the critics? Don't be. We'll turn your meaningless tripe into a crock of art. Yes. Just send for the Avant Garde Playwriting Kit today and in no time at all, people will be saying things like this about your play.

JEFF. (*standing*) I haven't seen it, but I heard it was good.

JOHN. Send cash or public funds you want to pour down the drain to: All of the people some of the time, converted store front, anytown USA, that's All of the people some of the time, converted store front, anytown USA. (*All wave, with JEFF facing upstage.*)

LATIN AMERICAN TOUR

(*Lights up on JEFF doing crossword. He is wearing bald wig. At piano.*)

JEFF. Nine across. Let's see. A three letter word meaning "domesticated animal" beginning with C and ending with T. Boy *The Times* is sure getting obscure.

ROGER. (*enters 1 wearing hat and bald wig*) Hey, is this where they're auditioning for the Latin American Tour of "Annie"?

JEFF. Yeah, the sign-up sheet's over there. (*on piano*)

ROGER. You reading for Daddy Warbucks?

JEFF. If they ask me. You?

ROGER. I haven't made up my mind yet. (*signs in*) Hey, I'm number 287? What number are they up to?

JEFF. Four. I been here a long time and nobody's come through that door yet.

ROGER. Maybe they're out to lunch. (*cross to* L. *chair and sit*)

JEFF. Maybe they're coming back!

(*EVVIE heard singing in Spanish, enters 1 with sign in dialogue balloon: IGUANAS SALTARINAS.*)

EVVIE. Manana, manana, te amo manana . . .

JEFF. What's the sign say?

EVVIE. Can't you read Spanish?

JEFF. No.

EVVIE. It says "Leapin' Lizards." (*signing in*) I'm only number 288? That's not bad. Hey, aren't you guys too young to play Warbucks?

JEFF. Aren't you too big to play Annie? (*EVVIE cross to stool and sit.*)

EVVIE. No, Uta Hagen says: If you think small, you are small.

ROGER. Wait, I hear something.

JEFF. Maybe it's the casting director. (*Get ready. JOHN enters*

1 dressed with dog mask, enters panting with sign "Arfo.") Oh, my God . . .

ROGER. Hey, Fido, the paper's over there.

JOHN. For your information, I signed up three days ago. I'm number 59. They up to five yet? *(cross to R. chair, sit)*

JEFF. *(despair)* Nooo.

JOHN. How long you been waitin'?

JEFF. Samuel Beckett would have left by now.

EVVIE. *(reading trade paper)* Oh, no!

ALL. What, what??

EVVIE. *(reading)* "Casting for the Latin American Tour of 'Annie'. All principle parts are already cast. This is for chorus only."

JOHN. What about the dog?

EVVIE. They're using a chihuahua.

(Ad lib lines of anger pile on top of each other. ALL stand.)

ROGER. No lousy chorus part for me.

JEFF. No way!

EVVIE. I'd rather starve.

JOHN. I'm not gonna waste any more time here.

ROGER. *(in the clear)* Look, the door is opening!

JEFF. *(to EVVIE)* Gimme that sign.

ALL. No, me, me.

(ALL cross D. to imaginary door. ALL grab sign. "Manana, manana, te amo manana." Nobody comes.)

EVVIE. Nobody's coming.

JEFF. I smiled for nothing.

(ALL return to seats.)

MAKING THE ROUNDS

(JEFF playing the piano.)

EVVIE.
STOP MY ALARM, GIVE MY AGENT A CALL
I CHECK WITH MY SERVICE, BUT THAT ISN'T ALL

FEED THE CAT
PSYCHE MYSELF UP TO GO OUT
MAKIN' THE ROUNDS.

JOHN. (*cross to piano and play*)

GET TWENTY TOKENS AND PLENTY OF DIMES
STEAL ME A CROSSWORD FROM SOMEBODY'S TIMES

ALL. (*stand*)

THEN I'M OFF
HOPIN' TO CATCH THE NEXT TRAIN
MAKIN' THE ROUNDS

ALL.

SHUTTLES AND CHECKERS
(*cross D. to apron*)
AND CASTING DIRECTORS
AND WAITING ROOMS FOR WAITING AS WE PASS
   OUR MINUTES BY
MAKIN' THE ROUNDS. MAKIN' THE ROUNDS.
(*EVVIE to piano to play.*)

MEN.

GET OFF AT GRAND CENTRAL, AND RUN UP
   BROADWAY
(*men at stool*)
JUST TO DISCOVER THEY'VE GONE FOR THE DAY
GRAB A BITE

ALL.

YOGURT AND TEA ON THE BUS
MAKIN' THE ROUNDS, MAKIN' THE ROUNDS.

EVVIE. (*Men look at EVVIE.*)

SHUTTLES AND CHECKERS
AND CASTING DIRECTORS

ALL.

AND WAITING ROOMS FOR WAITING AS WE PASS
   OUR MINUTES BY
MAKIN' THE ROUNDS.

ROGER. (*Cross to piano and play. Others gather at piano.*)

THE CALL THAT I LEFT I GET BACK TO AT LAST
WHERE SOMEBODY TELLS ME

JEFF.

IT'S ALREADY CAST

ROGER.

I GO HOME OR MAYBE I TAKE IN A SHOW

ALL.

MAKING THE ROUNDS

I ADD IT ALL UP AS I FALL INTO BED
NO WORK TOMORROW AND I'M IN THE RED
GO TO SLEEP THO' I'M STILL OUT ON THE STREET
MAKIN' THE ROUNDS
MAKIN' THE ROUNDS
SHUTTLES AND CHECKERS
AND CASTING DIRECTORS
AND WAITING ROOMS FOR WAITING AS WE PASS
   OUR MINUTES BY
MAKIN' THE . . .

EVVIE. (*The following lines are all sung in unison until the end of the number*):
CALL THAT I LEFT I GET BACK TO AT LAST
WHERE SOMEBODY TELLS ME THE PART'S ALREADY
   BEEN CAST
THE CALL THAT I LEFT I GET BACK TO AT LAST
MAKIN' THE ROUNDS.

JEFF.
ROUNDS
MAKIN' THE ROUNDS, THE ROUNDS,
MAKIN' THE ROUNDS,
MAKIN' THE ROUNDS, THE ROUNDS . . .
MAKIN' THE ROUNDS, THE ROUNDS
MAKING THE ROUNDS
MAKING THE ROUNDS.

JOHN.
ROUNDS
SHUTTLES AND CHECKERS
AND CASTING DIRECTORS
SHUTTLES AND CHECKERS
AND CASTING DIRECTORS
SHUTTLES AND CHECKERS
AND CASTING DIRECTORS
MAKING THE ROUNDS.

ROGER.
CALL THAT I LEFT I GET BACK TO AT LAST
WHERE SOMEBODY TELLS ME IT'S ALREADY CAST
I ADD IT ALL UP AS I FALL INTO BED
NO WORK TOMORROW AND I'M IN THE RED
GET OFF AT GRAND CENTRAL AND RUN UP
   BROADWAY.
JUST TO DISCOVER THEY'VE GONE FOR THE DAY
MAKING THE ROUNDS.

AGENT

JEFF. (*as "Agent, Marty Gelt" at desk*) Sally, who's on line 5? Nancy? That pig-faced amazon? Put her on. (*on phone*) Hi, cutie. Listen, Nancy, they want you for the movie. I've got the producer, Sid Goldman, on another line. I'm going to ask a 100 grand and a percentage. Hold on, baby.

JOHN. (*enters 1 as "Actor"*) Hello, Marty. Long time no see.

JEFF. Hold on, just let me get this. (*on phone*) Sidney? Hi, Marty Gelt, here. Listen, Nancy's definitely interested in the part, Sid. What kind of monies are we talking about? Come on, Sid. You want the next Liza Minelli to work for peanuts? She's worth at least 100 grand. Alright, forget it. (*to JOHN*) What's up John?

JOHN. Nothing, Marty, I waited an hour and a half to see you. I've had this appointment for three months. I happen to be an exclusive client of yours, Marty.

JEFF. Hold on, just let me get this. (*on phone*) Nancy, I turned the job down for you. Forget about paying your rent. Yo're gonna be a big star or nothing. Trust me. (*hangs up*) Cow. You know, John, you're beautiful. I'm going to climb right over this desk and kiss you on the lips.

JOHN. You don't have to do . . .

JEFF. Hold on, just let me get this. (*on phone*) Gelt, who's this? Mickey? It's Mickey Rooney. Mickey, I adored you in Sugar Babies. Listen, bubbie, I got a new film script I want you to read. It's called "Andy Hardy Gets Sent to a Home" Mickey? Mick. (*hangs up*) Shrimp! You know something, John, you're going to be the next Tovah Feldshuh.

JOHN. That's what I want to talk to you about, Marty. Why am I only being sent out on parts for Jewish women?

JEFF. Look, I got your resume right here. I wrote it down. The next Tovah Feldshuh.

JOHN. Marty, that's my resume, but that's not my picture. That is Tovah Feldshuh.

JEFF. Oh yeah, now that I look at ya.

JOHN. Marty, what about commercials?

JEFF. Hold on, just let me get this. (*on phone*) Gelt, who's this? Tony, Tony Perkins. What, huh? Tony, get your mother off the phone, will ya? (*hangs up*) Psycho. You know John, I might have something for you right here on my desk. Yeah, can you look like a steelworker?

JOHN. Yeah, sure

JEFF. Nah, forget it. They're looking for a woman.

JOHN. A Jewish woman?

JEFF. Hold on, just let me get this. (*on phone*) Jane, Jane Fonda, wait, Jane, I can't hear you over the Nautilus machines. I'll get back to you later. Ciao, Baby.

JOHN. You know, if I hadn't done that porno film my kids would be starving. (*stand*)

JEFF. Hold on, just let me get this. (*phone*)

JOHN. I am becoming nationally known as Cowboy Johnny Bulge.

JEFF. Who's this? (*on phone*) Norman Lear, Baby. You're looking for a star for your new series. What do you need, Norman?

JOHN. I hate you! (*takes out gun*)

JEFF. (*describing Actor to a "T"*) A 30-ish Actor?

(*height*)

Young Leading Man

(*hair*) blonde, curly hair

Athletic build

Big Singing Voice?

Nah, sorry, Norman, I got nobody like that. (*Actor strangles Agent.*)

COMPOSER SKETCH

ROGER. (*at piano*) Da Da Da

That sounds good.

Da Da Da Da—That sounds great!

Da Da Da Dah Dah Daaah Daah (*Give My Regards to B'way.*) It's not coming. The second act is crying for a love song and it's just not coming. Inspiration is not with me today. Everything I write seems to have already been done. Done! (*sung:*) Done done done, done done done, done done done done done . . . (*William Tell overture*) I gotta be more careful. All I need is another lawsuit. Suit, coat pants, vest, mittens . . . (*sung:*) Glove me da da, Glove me da, da da da (*Aura Lee*). That's terrible. There must be something that can inspire me . . . a woman . . . Hey, what about Trixie, that waitress at the corner coffee shop . . . (*sung:*) I wish I were in Trixie . . . (*Dixie*) What am I doing? That's my opening number! I'm stealing from the stuff I already stole. That's sick . . . sick! Of course, now I know. It's her. She's been in the back of my mind all along . . . (*into COMPOSER TANGO*)

HUNGUP TANGO (COMPOSER TANGO)

(*ROGER at piano playing as "Patient."*)

ROGER.
I LOVE YOU, DOCTOR
YOU MEAN SO MUCH TO ME.
OTHER WOMEN SHARE MY BED
BUT IT'S YOU WHO SHRINKS MY HEAD
AND YOU DO IT FOR A REASONABLE FEE.
(*spoken*)
And then she sings . . .

(*EVVIE enters 1 as "Doctor." Cross down to mark A.*)

EVVIE.
YOUR CASE IS CLASSIC
YOUR FATHER MADE IT SO
HE WAS AN ARTIST
WHO MADE MONEY, BUT HE SIGNED HIS PAINTINGS
REMBRANDT AND VAN GOGH.
(*cross to L wall*)
ROGER.
MY FUTURE SEEMS SO BLEAK.
EVVIE.
THEN YOU SHOULD SEE ME MORE.
ROGER.
I COME THREE TIMES A WEEK.
EVVIE.
THEN WHY NOT MAKE IT FOUR?
ROGER.
I DO MY PRIMAL SCREAMS.
EVVIE.
HE SHUDDERS AND HE SWEATS.
ROGER.
I TELL HER ALL MY DREAMS.
EVVIE.
I PUT THEM ON CASSETTES.

(*EVVIE cross to piano.*)

ROGER.
YOU UNDERSTAND ME
  EVVIE.
I KNOW I DO
  ROGER.
IT'S MORE THAN I CAN BEAR
  EVVIE.
HE'S A VERY SICK BOY
  ROGER.
WE'VE HAD OUR UPPERS AND OUR DOWNS
DESPERATE CALLS FROM OUT-OF-TOWN
BUT THEY HAVEN'T PUT AN END TO OUR AFFAIR
  EVVIE.
I KNOW YOUR SECRETS
(*seated next to ROGER on his* R.)
IN ME YOU CAN CONFIDE
ALL YOUR HANGUPS WE'LL UNRAVEL
AN WE'LL ALWAYS TRAVEL SIDE BY SUICIDE
  BOTH.
IF YOU FEEL GUILTY
YOUR MUSIC'S NOT YOUR OWN.
JUST SHELL OUT SIXTY AN HOUR
  ROGER.
AND YOU'LL NEVER WALK. . . .
  BOTH.
BY YOUR SELF.

(*BLACKOUT*)

HUNS

(*JEFF enters 1 as prospective "Hun". EVVIE enters 2 as "Casting Director".*)

EVVIE. Next!
JEFF. (*with yell and cossack leap*) Ugh! (*play the* D.C. *area*)
EVVIE. That's right, you've made the final callbacks.
JEFF. (*Grunt — pleased.*)
EVVIE. As you now, Mr. Attilla is always on the lookout for fresh blood.

JEFF. (*Grunt — I know.*)

EVVIE. Of course that doesn't mean, however, that we take just anyone. We're looking for a few good huns.

JEFF. (*Grunt — That's me.*)

EVVIE. Now, what is your name again?

JEFF. Arrrgghh Uh-huh.

EVVIE. How is that spelled? Two Uh-huh's?

JEFF. Uh-huh.

EVVIE. Uh-huh. I'd like to introduce you now to one of our most illustrious warriors, Taras Vulva.

(*JOHN enters as "Taras Vulva".*) (*1*)

JOHN. (*grunt*)

EVVIE. That's right, Vulv. This is the new candidate, Mr. Uh-huh.

JOHN. (*shaking hands with "Hun"*) Hi, hun. (*cross to JEFF*)

JEFF. (*Grunt — What's with this guy?*)

EVVIE. I think it only fair to tell you, Mr. Uh-huh, that Vulv's approval is crucial to your success. You see, he has Mr. Attilla's ear.

(*"Vulv" flashes rubber ear. Cross* R. *to chair, sit.*)

JEFF. (*Grunt — I'm impressed.*)

EVVIE. Now, Mr. Uh-huh, let's get down to business. Tell us, how are you at sacking and pillaging?

JEFF. (*Grunt — Great, the best. Short grunts as tells each city he pillaged. Count out on fingers to pinky — "IH — IH".*)

EVVIE. Very impressive. How about rape?

JEFF. (*Grunt — Wait till you see this. Begins to undo belt. Vulv moves in. Casting Director stops him. Return to* R. *chair.*)

EVVIE. No need to go any further. We have been having some trouble lately with the barbarians from Great Britain. How do you feel about Anglo-Saxons?

JEFF. (*Grunt — Hate them. Chops off imaginary head, slurps blood. Grunt — Want some?*)

EVVIE. No, thank you, I've had mine today. Did you bring a classical piece with you?

JEFF. (*Grunt — Of course. Gets up.*)

EVVIE. Would you do it please? (*cross* R. *— stand near JOHN*)

JEFF. (*Takes pose. Grunts — But soft, what light on yonder window breaks. Tis the east and Juliet is the sun.*)

EVVIE. . . . Arise, fair sun and kill the envious moon.
JEFF. (*Grunt — You know it?*)
EVVIE. Yes, I know it. It's one of my favorites. What is your vocal range? (*cross L. to JEFF*)
JEFF. (*Grunt — A to E-flat.*)
EVVIE. Can you tap?
JEFF. (*tap with hand on piano*)
EVVIE. Very good.

(*VULV whispers suspiciously to CASTING DIRECTOR. Cross to each other.*)

EVVIE. Your name is not really Uh-huh, is it? (*cross to JEFF D.C.L.*)
JEFF. Uh-uh.
EVVIE. You're a British spy, aren't you?
JEFF. Oh, how did you guess I was British?
EVVIE. (*take to VULV*) Because we are British, too.
JEFF. How do I know that? Say the password.
EVVIE and JOHN. Masterpiece Theatre.
JEFF. Jolly good. Nice to see you. I think this calls for a witty ditty, don't you? (*All shake hands.*)

(*EVVIE cross to piano to play, JOHN stand L. of piano. JEFF starts on mark A.*)

BRITISH

JEFF.
EVERYTHING IS ABSOLUTELY BETTER WHEN IT'S
    BRITISH
WHETHER COMEDY OR TRAGEDY, IT'S BETTER FROM
    ABROAD.
YES, AND EVERYONE WHO'S ANYONE IS BRITISH
    THROUGH AND THROUGH,
INCLUDING, I SUSPECT, OUR LORD.

FROM SOCIAL CONSCIENTIOUSNESS TO SILLY
    BEDROOM FARCE
(*cross L.*)
THE ENGLISH ALWAYS WRITE THE BETTER PLAY
WE'LL GIVE YOU QUITE A THOROUGH LICKING FROM
    YOUR MOTHER TONGUE

AFTER ALL, WHOSE LANGUAGE IS IT ANYWAY?
ALL.
WE'LL MAKE YOU LAUGH, WE'LL MAKE YOU SOB.
AMERICAN ACTORS WILL HAVE NO JOBS.
WE SET THE STANDARDS, WE ARE THE GUAGE:
RULE BRITANNIA, BRITANNIA RULES THE STAGE
QUITE SO (RADA, RADA, RAH-RAH RADA).
JEFF.
ACTORS WHO CAN ACT ARE ALWAYS INFINITELY
  BRITISH
(*cross* R.)
WHICH IS WHY WE'RE OFTEN SUMMONED HERE TO
  STAR IN BROADWAY SHOWS
YOUR PRODUCERS MAY HAVE MONEY BUT YOUR
  ACTORS GOT NO CLASS
I MEAN YANKEES DOING SHAKESPEARE SOUND LIKE
  RUTTING BUFFALOES.
ALL.
WE CAN FENCE AND RIDE AND DAZZLE YOU
WITH OUR ABILITY TO ADAPT TO ANY STYLE
USING SLICK TECHNIQUE AND A CONDESCENDING
  ACCENT
WE WILL NEVER FAIL TO MAKE A PILE.

WE'LL MAKE YOU LAUGH, WE'LL MAKE YOU SOB.
(*JEFF cross up to piano.*)
AMERICAN ACTORS WILL HAVE NO JOBS.
WE TRILL OUR PROSE WITH TRAINED CHORDS
RULE BRITANNIA, BRITANNIA RULES THE BOARDS
BRITANNIA RULES, BRITANNIA, BRITANNIA RULES
  THE BOARDS.

(*FADE OUT*)

INTERMISSION

(*EVVIE as "Woman" and JOHN as "Man" enter from opposite
  sides. EVVIE 2. JOHN 3. Both have Playbills.*)

JOHN. Evvie.
EVVIE. John.
JOHN. Hey, long time no see. (*cross to each other, play* D.C.)

EVVIE. This is wonderful. Do you realize it's been over ten years!

JOHN. Ten years.

EVVIE. Well, at least, since Northwestern University.

JOHN. "Uncle Vanya", remember?

EVVIE. Oh yeah, that was a terrific show.

JOHN. Ah, we were just kids then. What did we know?

EVVIE. Are you connected with this production?

JOHN. No, I'm working out in Flushing.

EVVIE. Oh, is there a dinner theatre out there? I didn't know that.

JOHN. No, I'm working for my dad.

EVVIE. Aren't you acting anymore?

JOHN. Well, there was a time there when nothing was happening. There weren't any decent parts and the old man offered to put me on the payroll. So what happens? After two weeks I'm promoted, I got fifteen guys working under me, a new car and a condominium. Listen, if you ever need any zippers, we make all kinds. So what about you? I bet with that voice of yours, you work all the time.

EVVIE. No, I haven't kept up at all really. Two children take up a lot of one's time.

JOHN. You got two kids?

EVVIE. Yes, John, I do. A boy and a girl.

JOHN. Is your husband here? I'd like to meet him.

EVVIE. No. For George the theatre is nothing but a high risk investment.

JOHN. You know, I've been thinking of getting back into it again.

EVVIE. Acting?

JOHN. Yeah, just gonna chuck it all and start making the rounds again, if Dad doesn't make me a vice-president pretty soon.

EVVIE. What do you think of this show we're seeing tonight?

JOHN. Terrific. Great.

EVVIE. Our old friend up there, Peter.

JOHN. He's wooden.

EVVIE. He always was. You were better than him. Remember, he only had a walk-on in "Uncle Vanya".

JOHN. Yeah, but he was always pushy. That's why he got the breaks. I could never do that.

EVVIE. Neither could I.

(*Lights blink twice. ROGER enters and sits piano.*)

ROGER. Curtain going up, folks.
EVVIE. Well, let's keep in touch, okay?
JOHN. You bet. Bye now.
EVVIE. Nice to see you again. Bye John.

(*They separate into two spots.*)

JOHN. I'll send you a gross of zippers, assorted.

(*They part, with lingering hands and glances. EVVIE crosses to
    mark A, JOHN to mark C, where they sing the song in
    spotlights.*)

COULD HAVE BEEN

(*ROGER playing piano.*)

EVVIE and JOHN.
SEND ME TWO TICKETS WHEN YOU GET TO
    BROADWAY
I CAN TELL MY FRIENDS THAT I KNEW YOU WHEN.
    EVVIE.
I COULD HAVE BEEN AN ACTRESS
I COULD HAVE BEEN A STAR
    JOHN.
I COULD HAVE BEEN A LEADING MAN
I COULD HAVE GONE SO FAR
    BOTH.
BUT CIRCUMSTANCES CAME ALONG
AND PUT ME THROUGH A CHANGE
IT WASN'T WHAT I HAD IN MIND I HAD TO
    REARRANGE MY LIFE.
    JOHN.
EVERYONE SAID THIS BOY'S GONNA MAKE IT
BORN TO THE STAGE, ANY FOOL CAN SEE
EVERYONE SAID THIS BOY'S GONNA MAKE IT
WISHFUL WORDS NEVER MEANT TO BE.

EVVIE.
EVERYONE SAID WHAT A SOPRANO
SHE SHOULD BE SINGING ON THE STAGE OF THE
 MET
EVERYONE SAID WHAT A SOPRANO
WHY DO I REMEMBER WHAT I WANT TO FORGET.
 BOTH.
SEND ME TWO TICKETS WHEN YOU GET TO
 BROADWAY
WILL YOU STILL REMEMBER ME THEN
SEND ME TWO TICKETS WHEN YOU GET TO
 BROADWAY
I CAN TELL MY FRIENDS THAT I KNEW YOU WHEN.
 JOHN.
EVERYONE SAID I HAD SUCH PROMISE
 EVVIE.
I WAS HEADING FOR A BRILLIANT CAREER
 BOTH.
EVERYONE SAID I HAD SUCH PROMISE
THINGS ARE NOT ALWAYS WHAT THEY APPEAR.
 BOTH.
SEND ME TWO TICKETS WHEN YOU GET TO
 BROADWAY
WILL YOU STILL REMEMBER ME THEN
SEND ME TWO TICKETS WHEN YOU GET TO
 BROADWAY
I CAN TELL MY FRIENDS THAT I KNEW YOU WHEN.
 EVVIE.
I COULD HAVE BEEN AN ACTRESS
I COULD HAVE BEEN A STAR
 JOHN.
I COULD HAVE BEEN A LEADING MAN
I COULD HAVE GONE SO FAR
 BOTH.
BUT CIRCUMSTANCES CAME ALONG
AND PUT ME THROUGH A CHANGE
IT WASN'T WHAT I HAD IN MIND I HAD TO
 REARRANGE MY LIFE
MY LIFE, MY LIFE, MY LIFE, MY LIFE.

(*Slow fade to black on last word.*)

CRIST AND PONTIUS PILATE

(*Lights up on JOHN as "Pontius Pilate." Sitting on stool.*)

JOHN. Next!

(*JEFF enters as "Crist." Gives picture and resume to Pilate.*) (*2*)

JOHN. Hello, I'm Pontius Pilate. Crist?
JEFF. Christ.
JOHN. (*shows picture to audience*) You don't look like your picture, Crist.
JEFF. No, I shaved it off for a commercial.
JOHN. Doing anything now, Crist?
JEFF. No, I just got back from forty days in the wilderness.
JOHN. That's a long time. Couldn't you break your contract?
JEFF. I was tempted.
JOHN. OK, you cause the lame to walk and the blind to see, you talk in tongues, . . . what's this? You turn water into champagne?
JEFF. Champale.
JOHN. Don't pad your resume, Crist. Have you done anything in Jerusalem, Crist? Something I might have seen?
JEFF. Yeah, I rode an ass through town last Sunday.
JOHN. Sorry I missed it.
JEFF. Oh, you missed it?

(*JOHN dies. JEFF tries to resurrect; fails.*)

JEFF. (*looking heavenward*) What's the matter?

(*JOHN is revived.*)

JOHN. Okay, so you do revivals.
JEFF. I did the Dead Sea Water Ballet.
JOHN. Big part?
JEFF. No, just a walk-on.
JOHN. Any representative roles?

(*JEFF holds up a bagel.*)

JOHN. That's it? OK, let's hear you sing. Hey Tony!

(*ROGER enters as "Tony." Sits at piano.*)

ROGER. Yeah, whatta you want?
JOHN. This is our accompanist, Antonio DeMentis. Crist.
JEFF. Hi, Tony.
ROGER. Hi, Chris.

(*JEFF puts music in front of ROGER. ROGER plays intro to "Hallelujah Chorus."*)

JEFF. (*positioned at tip of piano D*) Hal . . .
JOHN. (*interrupts*) Thank you. Next.
JEFF. Forgive him. He knows not what he does. (*cross L. of piano*)
JOHN. Who are you talking to?
JEFF. My Dad.
JOHN. Your Dad?
JEFF. Yeah, he's the producer.
JOHN. Why didn't you say so in the first place? Look. Just sign here. You don't have to read it. (*cross to piano, give clipboard*)
JEFF. Gee, Mister Pilate, does it really mean so much to know somebody?
JOHN. You bet your hot cross buns, kid. (*Both cross D.C.*)

GOOD CONNECTIONS

(*ROGER playing piano.*)

JOHN.
THOUGH AN ACTOR MAY LOOK LIKE APOLLO
HAVE A VOICE THAT IS CLEAR AS A BELL
    JEFF. (*bell*)
    JOHN.
IF HE HAS NO RELATIONS
IN OUR OPERATION
HE'S GOT AS MUCH CHANCE AS A SNOWBALL IN
    HELL,
    BOTH.
SNOWBALL IN HELL
YOU GOTTA HAVE GOOD GOOD GOOD CONNECTIONS

(*Cross up to get hats and canes, JOHN from 3, JEFF from 1.*)
PUTTING FAITH IN TALENT IS A COMMON MISTAKE
BETTER NOT FORGET THAT YOU NEED LOTS OF
  FRIENDS TO GET THAT
LUCKY BREAK
2,3,4,
GOOD GOOD GOOD CONNECTIONS
(*cross* D.)
WILL LEAD YOU ON TO FAME
  JOHN.
NO MORE COMPETITION,
  JEFF.
NO CATTLE CALL AUDITIONS
  BOTH.
WHEN YOU MENTION THAT HOLY NAME.
  JEFF. (*spoken*) Hey Mr. Pilate. (D. *of mark B in spot*)
  JOHN. (*spoken*) Yes, Mr. Christ.
  JEFF. (*spoken*) What do you get when you cross King Tut, a
water tap and the three wise men?
  JOHN. (*spoken*) I give up. What do you get?
  JEFF. (*spoken*) Pharaoh Faucet Magi
  BOTH.
IF YOU WANT
(*JEFF cross* R., *JOHN* L. *ROGER plays under tempo.*)
  JEFF. Hey, hey!
  ROGER. (*spoken*) I'll follow you.
  JEFF. (*spoken*) No, thanks. I have twelve already.
  JEFF.
IF YOU WANT TO BE SEEN BY THE EMPEROR
(*cross to mark B*)
WHEN YOU GET TO THE CITY OF ROME
  JOHN.
(THAT'S HOME.)
  JEFF.
PLEASE DON'T BE SELF-CONSCIOUS
  JOHN.
JUST TELL'EM YOU KNOW PONTIUS
  BOTH.
AND YOU WON'T END UP IN A COLD CATABOMB,
  COLD CATACOMB.
(*cross to mark A*)
YOU GOTTA HAVE GOOD GOOD GOOD CONNECTIONS

EVEN WITH SOME PEOPLE THAT YOU'D RATHER SEE
  DEAD
NOW CAESAR IS YOUR SAVIOR BUT AT LEAST
  YOU'LL NEVER CRAVE YOUR
DAILY BREAD.
(*grapevine* L.)
'CAUSE IF YOU DON'T HAVE THOSE GOOD
  CONNECTIONS
YOU'LL END UP IN DESPAIR
(*JEFF grapevine* L., *JOHN* R.)
  JOHN.
NON COMPOS MENTIS,
  JEFF.
A CARPENTER'S APPRENTICE
  BOTH.
YOU'LL NEVER MAKE IT, NO
(*cross to* D.C. *spot*)
DON'T FORSAKE IT, THO'
NEVER MAKE IT NO
(*Voice-Over of "God" – "That's my boy!"*)
WHERE.

(*Fade out on last word as they exit 2.*)

THEATRICAL OLYMPICS

(*Lights up on ROGER and JOHN upstaging each other a la
Carol Channing. JEFF and EVVIE enter and sit on the
piano.*)

JEFF. Ladies, and gentlemen, welcome to the 25th annual
Theatrical Olympics. What is it we're seeing here, Evvie?

EVVIE. These are the finals in the Carol Channing event, Jeff.
In it the actors must sing, dance and act while preventing any
other performer on stage from being seen.

(*JOHN and ROGER exit.*) (*2*)

JEFF. Earlier today the Russian contender, Olga Popov, was
disqualified when it was discovered that she actually was Carol
Channing. Evvie?

EVVIE. We are about to see the exciting semi-finals in Curtain Call Milking, and the first contender up on the boards is the Italian competitor, Rebobo Spinoza.

(*JOHN enters as "Rebobo," gesticulating.*) (*2*)

JEFF. What an entrance. He's no stranger to the stage. It's all in the wrists, isn't it, Evvie?

EVVIE. He makes it look easy, but in reality it takes a well-developed lumbar region and a whole lot of chutzpah to do this as well as he does.

(*JOHN exits.*) (*2*)

JEFF. Spectacular! And now it is time for an event I'm sure we're all looking forward to: Broadway All-Star Wrestling. (*JEFF exits.*) (*3*)

EVVIE. In this corner, the horribly deformed hero of the hit show "Elephant Man."

(*ROGER enters as Elephant Man.*) (*3*)

ROGER. Sometimes I think my head is so big because my show won three Tonies.

EVVIE. And in this corner, the pathetically paralyzed star of "Whose Life is it Anyway?"

(*JEFF drags JOHN out as paralyzed star.*) (*2*)

JOHN. Kill me, won't you kill me, please. I want to die.

JEFF. Alright, men, watch that trunk, no kicking.

(*bell*)

JEFF. And the match is on. (*ROGER cross to JOHN.*)
JOHN. You watch what I can do with my tongue.
ROGER. Stand up and fight, shorty.
JOHN. Hey, Dumbo, your shoe's untied.
ROGER. Uh-oh (*ROGER starts to shake and falls to knees.*)
EVVIE. What's happening to the Elephant Man, Jeff?
JEFF. His head's too heavy, Evvie. He's going down.

(*ROGER's head hits floor.*)

JEFF. One, two, three . . .

JOHN. I can still raise my head.

ROGER. I can't believe I'm doing this for peanuts.

(*JEFF finishes countdown.*)

JEFF. Ten! The Winner! There you have it, Broadway All-Star Wrestling!

(*JEFF picks up dead hand, drops it. ROGER drags JOHN Offstage.*) (*2*)

JOHN. Kill me. Won't you kill me, please.

ROGER. I hope you live forever, you putz.

EVVIE. I have a regrettable announcement to make at this time. There will be no award given for Plot Lifting this year.

JEFF. Oh, why not?

EVVIE. One of the judges invalidated the whole event because he thought "Dream Girls" and "Sophisticated Ladies" were the same show.

JEFF. Well, I guess that means the old record still stands. As you know, it was held by the show "Shenendoah: which lifted 250 lines and eight songs from the musical "Oklahoma!". We have some cheap thrills coming up now, don't we Ev?

EVVIE. That's right, and the contenders are waiting in their wings.

JEFF. First, from Broadway, the Martin Beck theatre in New York, Count Dracula.

(*ROGER enters—suave vampire.*) (*3, cross to mark C.*)

EVVIE. And from the Secaucus Community Theatre production, Count Dracula.

(*JOHN enters—ratty vampire.*) (*1, cross to mark A.*)

JEFF. Now, for the first time anywhere, we present the world premiere of the Freestyle Suck. Our own galant co-host volunteered to be the donor today.

EVVIE. I think my official title is Suckee. (*jump off piano, go to B*)

JEFF. I think you're right. The Jersey Vampire won the toss so he goes to bat first. (*JOHN cross to EVVIE, suck.*) That's the direct approach. Just look at that overbite. What a set of choppers! Uh-oh, he's slowing down. Yes, it looks like he's had enough.

(*JOHN belches and exits.*) (*1*)

JEFF. How was it, Ev?
EVVIE. Oh, he's an animal.

(*ROGER cross to EVVIE, suck.*)

JEFF. Well, I guess that leaves it up to you, Count. Look at the difference. Such nuance, such subtle nibbles. He's a professional alright. A quick fondle. Oh my God, he's opening his shirt. Could it be? Is it? Yes it is. It's a double suck! Look at that sucker go. I think we have a winner. Yes, we have a winner. Count? You won, Count. Count, you can stop now. Count (*holds up a cross*)

(*ROGER fades and exits.*) (*2*)

EVVIE. That was fun. Now, in a different vein, here are the results of the iambic pentameter and the 500 word mixed review.
JEFF. But coming up right now we have a special treat. If you've ever sat down front during a show, you'll know how important spittle projection is to an actor's performance.
EVVIE. The French in particular have developed this technique into a fine art. We are now going to watch the favorite in the "Hop Skip and Spit" event, Monsieur Jacques La Phlegm.

(*ROGER enters as Jacques.*) (*1*)

JEFF. Here's Jacques now, checking out the playing area, warming up for his attempt. His selection is from Moliere's "Would Be Imaginary School for Misanthropes." He's on his mark, the crowd is breathless in anticipation, and he's on.
ROGER. (*bound, bound, bound*) Aujourd'hui du Saint Louis, du deux soir et (*hock*) tui! (*cross from R. wall to D.C., spit*)
EVVIE. Spectacular.

(*ROGER exits.*) (*1*)

JEFF. I think we may have a record, Evvie.

EVVIE. Yes, seventeen tables.

JEFF. Amazing.

EVVIE. Well, that about covers everything, doesn't it, Jeff?

JEFF. At least all the people in the back there, Evvie.

EVVIE. As we draw near to the close of these games, we look forward to the exciting Finale in which the cast of "Children of a Lesser God" will put soot on their fingers and talk dirty.

JEFF. This is Jeff Haddow.

EVVIE. And Evalyn Baron, saying goodnight.

BOTH. And break a leg!

(*BLACKOUT*)

INTRODUCTION TO THEATRE PARTY LADIES

(*JOHN as "Jenny" enters into house.*)

JOHN. Dora, Edith, where are you girls? Excuse me, does anybody know where table XX is? They said it's behind a post somewhere's. Oh, you like my dress, do you? I got it on sale at K-mart. What are you drinking there? Coke? You know, I can't understand why anyone would want to put that stuff up their nose. The bubbles would make you sneeze.

(*JEFF as "Dora" enters into house.*)

JEFF. Jenny, where are you? Hi, honey. Are you sure this is a theatre?

JOHN. Well, I think so.

JEFF. Have you seen that show all about senior citizens?

JOHN. No, what's it called?

JEFF. Let my people gum. (*Go upstairs onto stage.*)

JOHN. I think our seats are up here. OOOh, you nasty man you. (*goosed*)

JEFF. What happened honey?

JOHN. You look out for that man there. He's a dirty old man.

JEFF. The one with the (*fill in description*)?

JOHN. Yeah, and the greasy hands.

JEFF. That's terrible. (*looks at man lewdly and wiggles*

tongue) We have this Schrafft's bill we have to settle. Oh, look, these people are smoking cigarettes with twisted ends. My grandson smokes that brand. Did you have the Cream Caramel Mountain Surprise?

JOHN. No, I surely didn't.
JEFF. Musta been Edith. What about the Banana Barge?
JOHN. The one with the prune topping.
JEFF. Yeah, that's the one.
JOHN. No, I didn't have that neither.
BOTH. Must have been Edith.

(*ROGER as "Edith" enters onto stage.*)

ROGER. Dora, Jenny, where are you girls?
ALL. Kisses, kisses. (*smack loudly*)
ROGER. Who's got the tickets?
JOHN. I do. It's table XX.

(*ALL cross to chairs on stage.*)

ROGER. I can't see a thing. Terrible.
JEFF. This must be wrong. This seat is rotten. There's a post there.
JOHN. No, no this will never do.

(*ALL attempt to exchange seats and end up in their original seats.*)

ROGER. Better, much better.
JEFF. Yes, Oh yes.
JOHN. This is good.

THEATRE PARTY LADIES

(*EVVIE at piano. ROGER, JEFF, JOHN are three ladies.*)

EVVIE. Would you please take off your hats!
LADIES. Shhhhhhhhhhhhhh!
ROGER. How rude!
LADIES.
WE'RE THE THEATRE PARTY LADIES

WE WILL SIT IN FRONT OF YOU
AND MAKE YOU GO INSANE.
WE ALWAYS BRING A LOT OF CANDY TO THE
  THEATRE
JUST TO RATTLE CELLOPHANE.
(*rattle, rattle*)
WE'RE IN LOVE WITH ALL THE ACTORS
AND OF COURSE MAX FACTOR'S LATEST MAKE-UP
  CRAZE.
WE'RE THE THEATRE PARTY LADIES
AND WE COME TO ALL THE MATINEES.

HATS AND FURS AND BOAS ARE BOPPIN DOWN
  BROADWAY
CHARTERED BUSSES SWINGIN' US IN FROM
  ROCKAWAY
WIDOWS, GRANDMAS, DIVORCEES,
COSTUME JEWELRY, CORSET STAYS,
SHOO BE DOO DAY
RAT A TAT TAT
CATCHIN' ALL THE PLAYS, UH-HUH
AT THE HELEN HAYES.
    JOHN.
I TALK TALK TALK ALL THROUGH THE PLAY
I LOVE THAT POINTLESS CONVERSATION
'BOUT MY BAD BACK OR MY DAUGHTER-IN-LAW
OR THE SCAR I GOT FROM MY OPERATION
    JEFF and ROGER. (*spoken*) Ooh, let's see it.
    ALL.
HATS AND FURS AND BOAS ARE BOPPIN' DOWN
  BROADWAY
CHARTERED BUSSES SWINGIN' US IN FROM OYSTER
  BAY
SISTERS OF THE CHURCH BAZAAR
B'NAI BRITH AND D.A.R.
SHOO BE DOO DAY
RAT A TAT TAT
GONNA SHOUT ENCORE ENCORE
AT THE BARRYMORE.
    JEFF.
I ALWAYS SIT IN THE MEZZANINE

I ASK MY NEIGHBOR, TELL ME DEAR
SHOULD I LAUGH OR SHOULD I CRY
BECAUSE YOU SEE I CANNOT HEAR.

ROGER. (*spoken*) Laugh.
JOHN. (*spoken*) Cry.
ALL.

HATS AND FURS AND BOAS ARE BOPPIN' DOWN
  BROADWAY
CHARTERED BUSSES SWINGIN' US IN FROM
  SHEEPSHEAD BAY
DIET PILLS FOR COMEDY
GERITOL FOR TRAGEDY
SHOO BE DOO DAY
WHAT DID HE SAY?
LOOKIN' FOR A MAN, UH-HUH
AT THE LUNT-FONTANNE.

JOHN.

I LOVE TO GO TO THE LADIES LOUNGE
I TAKE MY LIPSTICK AND COMPACT
I WAIT IN LINE FOR A VACANT STALL
IT'S MY FAVORITE SEAT FOR THE WHOLE SECOND
  ACT!

JEFF. (*spoken*) It's all that prune topping, Edith.
ALL.

HATS AND FURS AND BOAS ARE BOPPIN' DOWN
  BROADWAY
CHARTERED BUSSES SWINGIN' US IN FROM
  ROCKAWAY
WIDOWS, GRANDMAS, DIVORCEES,
COSTUME JEWELRY, CORSET STAYS

ROGER. (*spoken*) Look at them kiss. (*stand and point*)
JEFF. (*spoken*) Who's in this? (*stand and point*)
JOHN. (*spoken*) There goes the curtain. (*stand and point*)
JEFF. (*spoken*) Richard Burton?
ALL.

STOP THE SHOW WE'RE WALKIN' IN LATE
AT THE TOP OF THE VILLAGE GATE
WE'RE REALLY GETTING DOWN
IN MANHATTAN TOWN.

(*BLACKOUT*)

THE WARMUP GURU

(*JEFF enters as "Guru."*)

JEFF. (*from house onto stage, play whole stage at will*) Namaste, shanti, shanti, om, om, om. Why did the sacred cow cross the Ganges? Anyone? (*wait for audience response*) Sharp group. Allow me to introduce myself. I am Perfect Master Ka Ka Ji and I am going to teach you the esoteric doctrine of audience warmup yoga as it was taught to me by my teacher, the even more perfect Master Gah Li Ji. His most famous exercise was designed to increase the circulation in the hands and to develop the shoulders and the bicep region. The first thing I am going to be asking you to be doing is to be taking the left hand, that's this one and putting it behind the back like so. And to be taking the right hand, that's this one, and putting it out in front of your shoulder like so. Now it is very important for everyone to be doing this. (*No one does it.*) You know, sometimes I say to myself, you should get out of the guru business. Open a delicatessen. Call it the New Deli. Henny Youngman, 1947. It is very important to see some hands for illustration. Thank you. Alright, I want you to be moving that hand back and forth, back and forth in opposite directions very fast, very fast, when I say go. Ready? Go. Let me see them. Oh, that's very good. Namaste, shanti, om. Now that is what you have been doing for the first act. For the second act, I want you to be taking the left hand out from behind the back and putting it shoulder width apart from the first hand and moving both hands in opposite directions very fast, very fast when I say go. First we take this side of the house. Ready? Get ready. Get them up there, get 'em up. What's the matter, sir, you can't get 'em up? Ready, go. Thank you. Now this side, ready go. Thank you. This side you are very good. You are like Brahmin priest, you are close to Krishna. (*to other side*) This side, you have been eating meat. You cannot fool Ka Ka. But I am going to give you one more chance to get even with the other side of the house. We are going to do the exercise one more time. But this time we are going to use a visual aid. You will do the exercise when you see the Applause sign. Are you ready? Everybody get ready. Can you do it twice in one night, sir? Ready, go! (*holds up Hindi applause sign*) That's applause in Hindi. Thank you. Namaste, shanti, om. (*exit 2*)

(*Lights brighten for critic party doll.*)

CRITIC PARTY DOLL

(*EVVIE is the "Wife" and ROGER is the "Playwright" from Avant-Garde Playwrighting Kit. ROGER is glum. Enter from house.*)

EVVIE. What's the matter, honey? Critics got you down?

ROGER. Yeah, look, John Simon called my play a styrofoam turd.

JOHN. (*enters as "Announcer," from house*) Playwrights, choreographers, directors! Has your career been ruined by a snotty remark in the press? And you, you performers, tired of putting up with vicious personal insults? What have the critics called you?

JEFF. (*entering*) Stoop-shouldered Moron.

ROGER. Muscle-brained pretty boy.

EVVIE. Yenta.

JOHN. Now you can take your revenge on those vindictive bastards in the privacy of your own home with . . . (*JEFF goes offstage and gets doll, EVVIE positions stool as in diagram. JEFF enters with doll.*) The Critic Party Doll!! There are a thousand and one uses for this amazing cathartic sensation. You can slap him, punch him in the nose, hang him, burn him. Better yet break down his pretentious facade by putting him in the audience and forcing him to laugh, clap, and yell "Bravo!" Or better yet, put him up on stage, and you walk out during the first act. (*Actors follow directions for hitting, etc.*)

EVVIE. Lousy. (*cross away L.*)

ROGER. Saves me an hour in the parking lot. (*cross away R.*)

JEFF. You sing almost as well as Liv Ullman. (*JEFF exits.*)

JOHN. And, if you really want to get to him, criticize his writing.

ROGER. The thing I like about you is one doesn't have to be intelligent to understand your reviews. (*cross to doll*)

EVVIE. I love your notices because they're soft and so absorbant.

JOHN. You can pretend he's Clive Barnes . . .

ROGER. "Is it British? I love it."

JOHN. or that in-depth reviewer Gene Shallit . . .

EVVIE. "This show sucks."

JOHN. or whoever it is that writes Rex Reed's reviews. Act now and your Party Doll will come with these bonus extras. Now (*ROGER get kit from offstage.*) you can get him where he's always gotten you. Now you can bomb him! (*ROGER holds up bomb.*) Pan him! (*EVVIE holds up pan. ROGER holds up giant screw.*) No need to explain that one. Send for your Critic Party Doll now. Write to:

Eye for an Eye Rubber Goods

Vengeance, Arizona

Or call? 6969696969696. That's 6969696969696. Do it today!

(*BLACKOUT*)

LOVE IN THE WINGS

(*EVVIE at piano. ROGER enters 1 and joins her.*)

ROGER.
WE MET AT THE START OF A LATE CASTING CALL
EVVIE.
I WASN'T SURE IF I LIKED HIM AT ALL
'CAUSE I WANTED A MAN WITH HIS FEET ON THE
    GROUND
ROGER.
ONLY A FOOL WANTS A LOVER WHO'S NEVER
    AROUND.
I MADE A DATE OUT OF BOREDOM NO LESS
EVVIE.
EQUALLY BORED I ANSWERED HIM YES
THE EVENING WAS AWFUL
ROGER.
AND SO WAS THE SHOW
BOTH.
WE FELL IN LOVE, JUST HOW WE NEVER WILL
    KNOW.
I WANT YOU TO KNOW THERE ARE EASIER THINGS
THAN BACK STAGE ROMANCES WITHOUT ANY
    STRINGS
I'LL NEVER MAKE PROMISES I CAN'T FULFILL
BUT YOU SHOULD KNOW THERE IS STILL
LOVE IN THE WINGS

EVVIE.
HE NEVER HAD MONEY TO GET THROUGH THE DAY
    ROGER.
NIGHTS WHEN I NEEDED HER, SHE WAS AWAY
WHEN YOU WENT ON A TOUR I KNOW WE WERE
    THROUGH
    BOTH.
WE GOT BACK TOGETHER, WHAT FOR, THAT'S A
    MYSTERY TOO
I WANT YOU TO KNOW THERE ARE EASIER THINGS
THAN BACK STAGE ROMANCES WITHOUT ANY
    STRINGS
I'LL NEVER MAKE PROMISES I CAN'T FULFILL
BUT YOU SHOULD KNOW THERE IS STILL
LOVE IN THE WINGS.

(*ROGER shows off on piano. EVVIE stops him.*)

    EVVIE.
HE WORKED AND I DIDN'T. IT WASN'T IDEAL
    ROGER.
IN ROMANTIC ROLES YOU WERE OVERLY REAL
THOSE ACTORS YOU KISSED I TOOK IT TO HEART
    BOTH.
WHO CAN SAY WHY? BUT SOMEHOW WE CAN'T
    STAY APART.
    BOTH.
I WANT YOU TO KNOW THERE ARE EASIER THINGS
THAN BACK STAGE ROMANCES WITHOUT ANY
    STRINGS
I'LL NEVER MAKE PROMISES I CAN'T FULFILL
BUT YOU SHOULD KNOW THERE IS STILL
LOVE IN THE WINGS

I WANT YOU TO KNOW THERE ARE EASIER THINGS
THAN BACK STAGE ROMANCES WITHOUT ANY
    STRINGS
I'LL NEVER MAKE PROMISES I CAN'T FULFILL
BUT YOU SHOULD KNOW THERE IS STILL
LOVE IN THE WINGS.
(*embrace*)

(*BLACKOUT*)

STANISLAW GOWUMPKI

(*JEFF enters 1 as "Stanislaw" sweeping, whistling. JOHN at piano.*)

JOHN. Hi, Stan.

JEFF. John, you're here late tonight. Would you mind to move your pedal foot? Do you know if Roger is still in his dressing room?

JOHN. I think so, Stan.

JEFF. Good, good. I finish dis later. (*walks to proscenium, knocks*) Roger, it's Stanislaw. Can you come out for a minute? I've got something for you.

ROGER. (*entering 1*) Hi, Stan. What's up?

JEFF. That girl was here again tonight. (*Both cross to A.*)

ROGER. Which one?

JEFF. You know which one. She gave me dis to give to you. (*gives him one long-stemmed red rose*)

ROGER. She's very special, Stan.

JEFF. I can tell there's something different about you.

ROGER. You can?

JEFF. Yes, I was once an actor myself. (*JEFF cross to D. of piano.*)

ROGER. You were?

JEFF. Yes. In Poland a long time ago. I played all the classic parts. The name of Stanislaw Golumpki was a household word. You should have seen me do Hamlet in Cracow. (*picks up broom*) Oto, Biedni Yorick. Yago znowem, Horatsio. One night after the show a beautiful girl came backstage just to shake my hand and I fell heels over head for her. And I vass worried, like you, dis crazy romance would take me away from the stage. But it didn't. We got married and we were very happy.

ROGER. Then why did you stop acting? (*ROGER cross to C.*)

JEFF. (*cross R. to A.*) Why? The war came, that's why. We were lucky. We managed to get to America, but it's not so easy to be an actor here when you can only speak Polish. I had nothing . . . except that beautiful woman I met in Cracow, and because of her, it didn't seem so bad that I wasn't a great actor anymore. And you know something? Dis year we are celebrating our forty-first wedding anniversary. Take it from old Stan. (*pointing to rose*) The career goes up, the career goes down, but love is always terrific. Have a good night, now. (*exits*) (*1*)

ROGER. You too, Stan. (*cross D. of stool*)

ONLY ONE DANCE

MY WORK IS MY EVERYTHING
MY SOUL MY VERY DEFINITION
BUT YOU ASK ME TO LET MYSELF GO
SHOULD I DANCE TO YOUR MUSIC
SHOULD I GIVE MYSELF TO YOU

YOU HAVE A SPECIAL BEAUTY
A SMILE THAT'S RARE TO SEE
A MIND BOTH SHARP AND FUNNY
I CAN'T RESIST YOUR SUDDEN MYSTERY.

ONLY ONE DANCE WITH YOU
AND I'D BE LOSING MYSELF
DELIGHTED BY THE DANCE YOU DO
SHOULD I GO DANCE WITH YOU
OR SHOULD I GO IT ALONE
WILL I EVER KNOW LOVE
IF I DON'T SURRENDER
TO YOUR DANCE AND YOU

WHAT HAPPENS IF I LOVE YOU
WILL I REMAIN THE SAME
SING THE SONG AS WELL OR BETTER
CHANGE THE LUCK I NEED TO PLAY THE GAME?

ONLY ONE DANCE WITH YOU
AND I'D BE LOSING MYSELF
DELIGHTED BY THE DANCE YOU DO
SHOULD I GO DANCE WITH YOU
OR SHOULD I GO IT ALONE
WILL I EVER KNOW LOVE
IF I DON'T SURRENDER
TO YOUR DANCE AND YOU

(*cross to stool*)

YOU HAVE ALL THE PERFECT WAYS TO REARRANGE
   ME
BUT WILL YOU STILL WANT ME THEN AFTER
   YOU'VE CHANGED ME?
WILL YOU WANT WHAT I WOULD BE?

ONLY ONE DANCE WITH YOU
AND I'D BE LOSING MYSELF
DELIGHTED BY THE DANCE YOU DO?
ONLY ONE DANCE WITH YOU
OR SHOULD I GO IT ALONE
WILL I EVER KNOW LOVE
IF I DON'T SURRENDER
WILL I EVER KNOW LOVE
(*cross to* C.)
SHOULD I LET IT HAPPEN
IS IT TIME NOW TO SURRENDER TO
THE DANCE AND YOU.

(*BLACKOUT*)

INTRODUCTION TO NO SMALL ROLES

(*EVVIE crosses to* C.S.)

EVVIE. Imagine, if you can, a hot summer's night in New York City's Central Park. Shakespeare in the Park. A production of JULIUS CAESAR. When onto the stage walks a lone spear carrier.

(*EVVIE exits as JOHN enters. EVVIE exits 3, JOHN enters 1, crosses to mark B, spotlight.*)

NO SMALL ROLES

(*JOHN enters as "Spearcarrier" in heavy armour. Speech is all done by JEFF as a voice-over. In spotlight at mark B.*)

JEFF. (v.o.) I can't believe the Romans really wore this stuff especially in the summer. No wonder they lost the Empire. At least it's nice being here in the park every night. (*sound of mosquito*) Oh, god, it's under my breast plate. (*sound of slurping*) That's gonna itch. This is my big act, where I have my line. Four years of college and two years of graduate school for one line. Why don't they just shut up and stab him. Everybody knows the story. Look at that Cassius. He's supposed to have a lean and hungry look so they cast a three-hundred pound Mexican. Here he goes with my favorite line: (*off*) "The fawlt dear Brutoos eez not in our starss, but een ourselfs dat we are underwear." That's what happens when you learn the part phonetically. Uh-oh he's got trouble with his body mike. Can't hear a thing. (*Sound: feedback, buzz, "Breaker 1-9, Breaker 1-9 I need a traffic report on the . . ." beep.*) No, it's OK. Arrgh, there's the itch and I can't move. What did the director say? (*with fey lisp*) "A Centurian never flinches . . ." Is that my cue? Was that my line? No, no, I'm OK. Boooring. 1,2,3,4,5,6, etc. . . . 25. There are 25 bald people in the audience. Hey, there's the agent I invited. He's looking at me. Oh, boy, I can see him! Oh, no, I can see him. I forgot to take my glasses off. How could I spend 30 minutes in front of a mirror getting into character and forget to take off my glasses. (*reaches for them*) Wait, if I take them off now everyone will notice. Well, what am I worried about? The Romans had glass they had metal. Wait, here comes my line. Here it comes . . . (*Said by JOHN onstage.*) Sail Heaser! (*Voice over con't.*) Shit, shit, shit, shit, shit! One lousy line and I blew it. (*sound of mosquito*) At least I'm working. (*sound of slurping*)

(*Lights fade slowly with slurping.*)

CHILD STAR

(*EVVIE enters dressed as a little girl and carries a teddy bear.*)

ROSES RED VIOLETS BLUE
LOTS OF LOLLIPOPS JUST FOR YOU
MIRROR MIRROR ON THE WALL
WHO'S THE PRETTIEST ONE OF ALL?

(*EVVIE tears the head off the bear and reveals a rock star costume underneath her little girl garments.*)

I'M THE GREATEST-LOOK AT ME
BEEN ON THE STAGE SINCE I WAS THREE
EVERY WEEK I MAKE LOTSA DOUGH
BUT I'M UP THE CREEK IF I START TO GROW

(*ROGER, JOHN, JEFF enter as rock backup.*)

UP THE CREEK, SHE'S UP THE CREEK

EVVIE. (*chorus*)
I'M SO SLICK I MADE IT TOO QUICK
I'M A CHILD STAR, CHILD STAR
I'M SO COOL WHO NEEDS SCHOOL
I'M A CHILD STAR, CHILD STAR
I DON'T CARE IF I CAN'T SPELL MY NAME.
EVVIE. (*spoken, ad lib*)
You spell it, you spell it.
EVVIE.
I'M INTO PILLS I'M SO NIFTY
GOTTA LOVER WHO'S PUSHIN' FIFTY
STRETCH LIMO AND A CHAUFFEUR BOY
I DON'T PLAY WITH THE AVERAGE KIDDIE TOY

(*chorus*)
I'M SO SLICK I MADE IT TOO QUICK
I'M A CHILD STAR, CHILD STAR
I'M SO COOL WHO NEEDS SCHOOL
I'M A CHILD STAR, CHILD STAR
SO WHAT IF THEY SAY THAT I'M A BITCH
EVVIE. (*spoken*) B-I-C-H-T
MY FRIENDS ALL HATE ME 'CAUSE I MADE IT BIG
GOT AN AGENT WHO'S A BIG BIG WIG
BACKUP.
UH - HUH
EVVIE.
NO STAGE MOMMA GONNA GIVE ME STRIFE
'CAUSE I TOOK OUT A CONTRACT ON HER LIFE
EVVIE. (*adlib*)
BREAK HER LEGS
BACKUP.
BOTH OF HER LEGS

(*chorus*)
I'M SO SLICK I MADE IT TOO QUICK
I'M A CHILD STAR, CHILD STAR
I'M SO COOL WHO NEEDS A SCHOOL
I'M A CHILD STAR, CHILD STAR
NOW THAT I'VE DONE EVERYTHING WHAT'S LEFT

EVVIE. (*adlib*)
WHAT'S LEFT, WHAT'S LEFT
   BACKUP.
DON'T THINK ABOUT IT, DON'T THINK ABOUT IT
DON'T THINK ABOUT IT, DON'T THINK ABOUT IT.
   EVVIE. OK, OK,

(*chorus*)
I'M SO SLICK I MADE IT TOO QUICK
I'M A CHILD STAR, CHILD STAR
I'M SO COOL WHO NEEDS SCHOOL
I'M A CHILD STAR, CHILD STAR
I'M NO FOOL I'M LIVIN' FOR TODAY.
   BACKUP.
CHILD STAR, BITCH, BITCH, BITCH
CHILD STAR, BITCH, BITCH, BITCH
CHILD STAR, BITCH, BITCH, BITCH
CHILD STAR, BITCH, BITCH, BITCH
(*EVVIE beats up the backup group.*)
   EVVIE. I WAS BAD.

SHAM DANCING

ROGER. (*by piano*) In our business, the triple-threat performer, that is the actor-singer-dancer has always been in cons-
tant demand. With CHORUS LINE and DANCIN' monopoliz-
ing talents of so many actor-singer-dancers, producers have been
left with no alternative. They hire actors and singers (*EVVIE 2,
JEFF 3, JOHN 1 enter.*) and use them in such a way that they
appear to (*Actors attempt ballet exercise in vain.*) be dancing.
Unfortunately, most of these non-dancers tend to move as slug-
gishly as Orson Welles after eating three meals at Luchow's. A
method of choreography has emerged whose lofty goal is to
make these clodhoppers look like budding Baryshnikovs. We
refer, of course, to the art of sham dancing. There are several
basic forms of sham dancing. (*Cross to mark B JOHN L., EV-
VIE C., JEFF R., in a line.*) The knee slap. (*Music, the group
does it.*) The bounce. (*Music, the group does it.*) The walk.
(*Music, the group does it.*) The brisk walk. (*Music, the group
does it.*) And the run. (*Music, the group does it. Music stops,
the group pants and gasps.*) The run is often followed by the

sweat and the gasp. For Sham Dancing's least strenuous technique, the dancers plant their feet firmly on the stage and rely entirely on verbal movement. (*JOHN at A, EVVIE, B, JEFF, C.*)

(*Music. The group sings and moves without moving their feet.*)

GROUP.
GOTTA DANCE! GOTTA WALTZ TO THE MOON.
GOTTA LEAP! GOTTA TAP TO THE TUNE.
ROGER. Often, the blatant incompetence of the sham dancers demands that audiences' attention be directed elsewhere. In a soft shoe or tap dancing sequence, imaginative lighting can be used.

(*Music. Lights out. EVVIE and ROGER use flashlights while tapping sound is heard. Lights up. JOHN and JEFF are caught rapping the floor with tap shoes on their hands. DS., split C.*)

ROGER. Sham Dancing has even borrowed from ballet. To give your number a spectacular finish, you try a lift. (*EVVIE does ballet moves. Music. Men try to lift EVVIE.*) Sham Dancing has sometimes exploited unusual gimmicks such as Tommy Tune's Boot Dance from BEST LITTLE WHOREHOUSE IN TEXAS and Michael Kidd's Whip Dance from DESTRY RIDES AGAIN. This evening we present a classic of sham dancing, originally written for the 1928 Broadway musical, WHOOPEE, Ladies and Gentleman, the Whoopie Cushion Dance. (*All line up, D. From R. to L., JEFF, EVVIE, JOHN, ROGER.*)
(*Music.*)
EVVIE. (*Fart, fart.*)
MEN. (*Fart, fart.*)
(*Music.*)
EVVIE. (*Fart, fart.*)
MEN. (*Fart, fart.*)
(*Music.*)
EVVIE. (*Fart, fart.*)
MEN. (*Fart, fart.*)
(*Music.*)
ALL.: (*FART.*)

(*BLACKOUT*)

INTRODUCTION TO ELIZABETHAN DINNER THEATRE

(*Play whole stage at will.*)

EVVIE. This is my favorite part of the show because I get to spend a few moments with you and ask for your help. This is the part of the show when we need suggestions from the audience. And the first suggestion we need is for an historical period. Anyone? (*Audience suggests. Actress repeats.*) Great. The second suggestion we need is for a place. Around the house, the world. (*Audience suggests. Actress repeats. Again, loudly for the men who say "Thank you."*) I hope you don't think we're going to do that for you now. We may be crazy, but we're not stupid. A previous audience gave us Elizabethan and dinner theatre. So I would like to cordially invite you to our Elizabethan Dinner Theatre. (*exits*) (*1*)

ELIZABETHAN DINNER THEATRE

JEFF. (*Entering 1 as "Waiter."*) Hello, sir. I'm your waiter Rustic Cretin.

JOHN. (*Entering 2 as "Edmund," a customer.*) I have a reservation for dinner and the show. The name is Edmund.

JEFF. Edmund? (*stares at JOHN*)

JOHN. Don't leer.

JEFF. Right this way, sir. (*aside*) Bastard.

JOHN. What is the show tonight? (*cross to chair sit*)

JEFF. Timon of Athens, sir. (*cross to table*)

JOHN. Well, I hope at least the dinner is good.

JEFF. For appetizers we have Romeo and Juliet goose pate. We use only the best star-crossed livers.

JOHN. Is it fresh?

JEFF. Right here on the premiese, we murder most fowl.

JOHN. What's the Shakespeare platter?

JEFF. Delicious, sir. I'd recommend the Richard III Special.

JOHN. What is that?

JEFF. Hump roast Olivier.

JOHN. Comes with gamey leg?

JEFF. That's the one.

JOHN. Wait, what's the Othello?

JEFF. That's Venetian Moor.

JOHN. Oooh, I'm a Moor connoisseur. Is it pure?

JEFF. Sure. Just a minute. (*calls offstage*) Any Moor? No Moor.

JOHN. You're sure there's no more pure Moor? What a bore.

JEFF. It's a discomfiture, but I'm absolutely sure that there is no more pure Moor. Could you endure our demure soup du jour?

JOHN. A broth by my troth?

JEFF. A consomme devoutly to be dished.

JOHN. Me thinks I'll try the Twelfth Night meatloaf.

JEFF. I'd not recommend that, sir.

JOHN. And why not?

JEFF. I had it yesterday and all night I was passing strange.

(*EVVIE enters 2 as "Lady Macbeth" washing her hands.*)

EVVIE. Would you have a wash and dry? (*cross D.*)

JEFF. All out, sorry. Come again.

EVVIE. Out, out damned spot.

JOHN. We should have done the (*Audience selection from introduction.*)

JEFF. (*to EVVIE*) I couldn't agree more. (*EVVIE exits 3.*)

JOHN. Moor?

JEFF. No more.

JOHN. What kind of meat is in the Chef Salad for dancers?

JEFF. Tutu salad flesh.

JOHN. Methinks I'll have a Western Hamlet and a Wittenberger.

JEFF. Right, sir. That comes with a vegetable. You get your choice of two from column A or two from column B.

JOHN. Two B's. No, not two B's.

JEFF. (*noting audience response*) How sharper than a serpent's tooth it is to have a thankless audience.

JOHN. I think someone's passing strange out there.

JEFF. Would you like a beer, sir?

JOHN. I'm not dead yet.

JEFF. Oh, that's very good, sir. I don't care what they think.

JOHN. I'll have a glass of Iago Sangria.

JEFF. You stall, I'll pack. (*JEFF exits.*) (*2, gets platter and dome.*)

JOHN. (*smoking a joint*) A hit, a palpable hit.

JEFF. (*returning with tray upon which a platter and dome*)

JOHN. What's this?

JEFF. It's your dinner, sir.

JOHN. But I ordered from the Shakespeare platter.

JEFF. Sorry, sir. All we have tonight is Bacon. (*lifts dome revealing head of ROGER as "Bacon," garnished*)

(*BLACKOUT*)

INTRODUCTION TO
HAVE YOU EVER BEEN ON STAGE . . .

(*In spotlight at B.*)

JEFF. One thing we haven't covered in the show so far is opera. Sure, we could do a parody of an opera but we've decided to do something a little less obvious. Our own Evalyn Baron (*EVVIE enters 2.*) is an accomplished lyric soprano and she is now going to sing a very pretty aria for us, "Un Bel Di" from Puccini's MADAME BUTTERFLY. Besides it's in her contract and we have no choice. (*JEFF exits.*) (*2*)

(*EVVIE starts singing ARIA. Stagehand puts Duck onstage. EVVIE sings in spotlight at mark B. After several measures, the Duck comes on from 1. EVVIE sees Duck as full stage lights come up. In horror, she crosses to JOHN, who plays intro to song. EVVIE sings and reacts to audience and Duck, etc.*)

HAVE YOU EVER BEEN ON STAGE . . .
(WITH AN ANIMAL)

(*JOHN playing piano. Starts intro, two times. EVVIE sings and reacts to whatever HERMIONE the Duck, does.*)

EVVIE.
HAVE YOU EVER BEEN ON STAGE WITH AN ANIMAL
I CAN TELL YOU AS AN ACTRESS THERE'S REALLY
NOTHING WORSE

YOU WILL ALWAYS BE UPSTAGED BY AN ANIMAL
THEY'RE FOREVER DOING SOMETHING
LIKE QUACKING IN THE MIDDLE OF YOUR VERSE

NEVER GO ONSTAGE WITH AN ANIMAL
THEY'RE DIFFICULT TO WORK WITH TAKE MY WORD
  IT'S TRUE
FOR, IF YOU GO ON STAGE WITH AN ANIMAL
YOUR CAREER WITH SUFFER DEARLY
THE DUCK WILL GET THE LAUGHS AND NEVER YOU
ANIMALS HAVE SUCH APPEAL
SO SPONTANEOUS AND SO REAL
SO NATURAL, SO CUTE, THEREFORE
I THINK I'LL NAIL HER FEET TO THE FLOOR

NEVER GO ONSTAGE WITH AN ANIMAL
LET THEM ALL RUN WILD OR LOCK THEM IN
  A CAGE
FOR NOTHING STEALS YOUR SCENE LIKE AN ANIMAL
THEY WILL SPOIL YOU FINEST MOMENT
BY LEAVING A DEPOSIT ON THE STAGE
ANIMALS CAN SPELL DEFEAT
WHEN THEY PAUSE TO BE INDISCREET
THEY CAN MAKE AN ACTRESS SEEM A SHAM
I REFUSE TO SHARE THE STAGE WITH A WEB
  FOOTED HAM

OH, NEVER GO ONSTAGE WITH AN ANIMAL
NOTHING COULD BE WORSE FOR A GENUINE ARTISTE
YOU'RE ALWAYS SECOND BILLING TO AN
  ANIMAL
YOU'LL FORGIVE THIS ENDLESS BITCHING
BUT THERE'S NOTHING SO BEWITCHING AS A BEAST

DON'T GET STUCK LIKE A CLUCK NEVER GO ON THE
  STAGE
WITH . . . A DUCK.

(*Fast fade as EVVIE exits 2 with Duck in her hands.*)

ADVICE TO PRODUCERS

(*JOHN at piano. JEFF and ROGER turn signs. JEFF 3, EVVIE 2, ROGER 1.*)

SIGN. Advice to Producers
ROGER.
IF YOU HAVEN'T ANY TALENT
BUT YOU WANT TO DO A SHOW THAT WILL GO
JUST TAKE OUR ADVICE.
AND YOUR PLAY WILL REALLY SELL.
SIGN. Ignore Author's Intent.
EVVIE.
CHANGE THE BOOK, DISTORT THE MEANING
(*EVVIE and JEFF countercross.*)
WHEN THE HUMOR'S REALLY SPARSE
JEFF.
IT IT'S TRAGIC, MAKE IT COMIC
IF IT'S COMIC, MAKE IT FARCE
SIGN. Use Lots of Blood
ALL.
CUT SOME THROATS WITH SILVER RAZORS
GRIND YOUR VICTIMS DOWN TO SIZE
WHEN THE SCRIPT GETS DULL AND WORDY
BAKE THE BODIES INTO PIES.
JEFF. (*spoken*) God that's good.

(*ROGER at piano and JOHN at signs. JEFF at signs* R., *JOHN at signs* L., *EVVIE* U.C.)

SIGN. Jerk Tears
MEN.
HURRY UP AND EXPLOIT MISERY
STROKES AND CANCER, BIRTH DISEASE
MAKE BIG BUCKS WITH UGLY MUTANTS
ALL.
PASS THAT BOX OF TISSUES, IF YOU PLEASE.
EVVIE.
USE A WHOREHOUSE FOR YOUR SETTING,
SEXY SHOWS CAN BRING YOU LUCK

PUT SOME BOYS AND GIRLS TOGETHER
GET THEM HOT AND WATCH THEM . . .
ROGER. (*spoken*) Win a Tony.
SIGN. Preview Forever
JOHN.
IF YOUR SHOW'S A HOPELESS TURKEY
NEVER LET THE CRITICS COME
EVVIE.
SATURATE THE TV AIRWAYS
WITH A SONG THAT'S REALLY DUMB.
(*Plays dumb song from a lousy show.*)
SIGN. Cash in on Nostalgia
ALL.
REVIVALS ARE BOTH TRIED AND TRUE
THEY'RE THE SAFEST SHOWS TO BACK
WAVE THE OLD RED, WHITE AND BLUE
AND IF YOU'RE REALLY SMART.
JOHN.
YOU'LL CAST IT BLACK.
SIGN. Try to Imagine Evalyn is Black. We Know it's Difficult.
EVVIE.
TAKE MY HAND
I'M A STRANGER IN TIMBUKTU.
SIGN. To Hell with Theatre. Do a Concert.
ALL.
GET FOUR KIDS WHO LOOK LIKE BEATLES,
YOU WON'T EVEN NEED A SET
PETER ALLEN OR MINELLI
MIDLER COULD BE YOUR BEST BET

BOOK A SHOWPLACE LIKE THE URIS
THEN AT NIGHT YOU'LL SLEEP SECURE
ROD MCKUEN SURE CAN FILL IT.
JEFF and JOHN. (*spoken*) Don't serve art, serve warm manure.
SIGN. Put a Cheap Disco Beat under your Show Tunes.

(*Disco Rounds. Mock disco dance.*)

SHUTTLES AND CHECKERS
AND CASTING DIRECTORS

AND WAITING ROOMS FOR WAITING AS WE PASS
  OUR MINUTES BY
MAKING THE ROUNDS
SHUTTLES AND CHECKERS
AND CASTING DIRECTORS
AND WAITING ROOMS FOR WAITING AS WE PASS
  OUR MINUTES BY
MAKIN' THE RA-HA-HA-HOUNDS, MAKIN' THE
  ROUNDS,
MAKIN' THE RA-HA-HA-HOUNDS, MAKIN' THE
  ROUNDS!

SIGNS. Suggest Titles to Insure Success:

"Walter Kerr Loved It"

"An Evening with Laurence Olivier"

"New Play By William Shakespeare"

"The Fantasticks"

If All Else Fails

Put an Animal Onstage

SIGNS. If That Doesn't Work Get Neil Simon. If You Can't Afford Him. Steal.

ALL.

SNATCH A TUNE FROM RICHARD RODGERS
LYRICS LIFTED FROM COLE PORTER
SAY YOU WANT A TRAGIC HERO
ARTHUR MILLER'S MADE TO ORDER
GRAB A TWO STEP FROM BOB FOSSE
STEAL FROM SONDHEIM. WHY NOT?
STORIES YOU CAN GET FROM SHAKESPEARE
GOD KNOWS WHERE HE GOT THE PLOT.

IF YOU HAVEN'T ANY TALENT
BUT YOU WANT TO DO A SHOW
THAT WILL GO
JUST TAKE OUR ADVICE
GET A SHOW THAT'S COMPLETE
GET A SHOW THAT'S OFF-BEAT
GET A SHOW. GET A SHOW.
WE REPEAT
LIKE "SCRAMBLED FEET."

(*BLACKOUT*)

INTRODUCTION TO ONE HAPPY FAMILY

(*ROGER as "Composer" from 'Tango' at piano.*)

ROGER. I haven't written an encore. (*Taps in rhythm on piano to next line.*) I've got to write an encore. Something beautiful . . . (*sings to the tune of "Beautiful Dreamer"*)
BEAUTIFUL ENCORE
(*spoken*) Oh, no. If I don't get this encore written, I won't have enough money to feed my family. Family!

ONE HAPPY FAMILY

(*ROGER at piano.*)

ROGER.
WE ARE ONE HAPPY FAMILY
A BROTHERHOOD, A SYMPHONY
SHARING IN A CRY OF PLAYERS
PLAYING ON IN HARMONY

(*Under next four lines, JEFF & EVVIE are heard fighting backstage.*)

ROGER.
WHEN WE'RE DOWN WE'LL STICK TOGETHER
HELP EACH OTHER ON THE WAY
FOR SOME SUCCESS FOR MANY SADNESS
IT SEEMS LIKE MADNESS BUT THAT'S THE
  DUES WE PAY

(*JEFF & EVVIE enter 2.*)

THREE.
WE ARE ONE HAPPY FAMILY
A BROTHERHOOD, A SYMPHONY
SHARING IN A CRY OF PLAYERS
PLAYING ON IN HARMONY
  ROGER. (*spoken*) Where's John?
  JEFF. (*spoken*) There he is.

JOHN. (*spoken*) Give me a break; I want to go home and watch (*appropriate TV show*)

(*JEFF pulls JOHN onstage from house.*)

ALL.
WHEN YOU'RE FEELING SAD AND EMPTY
(*ALL gather at piano.*)
YOU'RE BACKED UP BY ALL THE REST
YOU'RE INSPIRED BY THOSE BEHIND YOU
AND YOU FIND YOU HAVE COME UP WITH YOUR BEST

EVVIE. (*spoken* D.S. *to audience*) We just want to thank you for being such a fantastic audience. After all, if it weren't for you out there, there'd be no reason for us to be out here. And you know, even though we kid around a lot, laugh at the business, we poke fun at ourselves, we really love what we do. (*The men are doing funny business behind her.*) We're dedicated to the theater and there's no place else we'd rather be than on-stage performing for you. (*EVVIE crosses back to piano.*)

ALL.
SEND ME TWO TICKETS WHEN YOU GET TO
   BROADWAY
WILL YOU STILL REMEMBER ME WHEN
SEND ME TWO TICKETS WHEN YOU GET TO
   BROADWAY

HAVEN'T WE SHARED SOME MAGICAL TIMES
AT STRATFORD ON AVON, THE GLOBE
REMEMBER THOSE NIGHTS AT THE MOSCOW ART
THE CURTAIN MAY FALL BUT WE'RE NEVER APART

I'M SO SLICK, I MADE IT TOO QUICK
I'M A CHILD STAR, CHILD STAR,
I'M SO COOL, WHO NEEDS SCHOOL, I'M A CHILD STAR

YOU GOTTA HAVE GOOD GOOD GOOD CONNECTIONS
FUTTING FAITH IN TALENT IS A COMMON MISTAKE
BETTER NOT FORGET THAT YOU NEED
LOTS OF FRIENDS TO GET THAT LUCKY . . .

WE'RE THE THEATRE PARTY LADIES
WE WILL SIT IN FRONT OF YOU AND MAKE YOU
GO INSANE

EVVIE.
WHEN IT'S ROUGH THERE'S NOTHING ROUGHER

(*JOHN exits.*)

ALL.
YOU CAN'T GO IT ON YOUR OWN
WITH FRIENDS AROUND YOU, YOU SOMEHOW TAKE
   IT
AND YOU MAKE IT. YOU'RE GLAD YOU'RE NOT

JEFF. (*spoken to EVVIE*) Bitch!

(*JEFF exits, EVVIE follows.*)

ROGER.
WE ARE ONE HAPPY FAMILY
A BROTHERHOOD, A SYMPHONY
SHARING IN A CRY OF PLAYERS
PLAYING ON IN . . .

(*JOHN 1, JEFF 3, EVVIE 2 stick heads onstage . . . in pinspots.*)

ALL.
HARMONY.

(*Slow fade on last syllable.*)

(*CURTAIN CALL*)

ALTERNATE BALLAD SKETCH

(*JEFF enters "1" as "Stanislaw" sweeping and whistling. ROGER is at the piano.*)

JEFF. Hi, Roger. (*polish word*)
ROGER. Hi, Stan. (*polish word*)
JEFF. Roger, you're here late tonight.
ROGER. Just foolin' around.
JEFF. How was the show?
ROGER. Packed to the rafters.

JEFF. Would you mind to move your pedal foot?

ROGER. Oh sure.

JEFF. Thank you very much.

(*JOHN enters "1".*)

JOHN. Excuse me.

JEFF. What are you doing here? Get out. You're not allowed.

JOHN. Would you give this to Hal Prince.

JEFF. No, you people drive me crazy. Go away.

JOHN. Thanks. Thanks for nothing.

JEFF. Wait! Come here. You're not from around here, are you?

JOHN. No.

JEFF. Where are you from?

JOHN. Tennessee.

JEFF. I knew it. I knew you talked kind of funny.

JOHN. You've got a good ear.

JEFF. I should. I was an actor once myself.

JOHN. You were?

JEFF. Yes. In Poland a long time ago. I played all the classic parts. The name Stanislaw Golumpki was a household word. I knew the Pope when he was an actor.

JOHN. How was he?

JEFF. It's a good thing he became a Pope. But I was really good. You should have seen me do Hamlet in Cracow. (*picks up broom*) Oto, Biedni Yorick. Yago znowem, Horatsio.

JOHN. Then why did you give up acting?

JEFF. Why? The war came, that's why. I was one of the lucky ones. I managed to get to America, but it's not so easy to be an actor here when you can only speak Polish. Ah — that was ancient history.

JOHN. I guess we're both sort of transplanted people.

JEFF. At least you can speak the language. Almost. And, God willing, there will be no war for you. Cheer up. Things will get better. Patience is a wonderful thing.

JOHN. My Daddy used to say that.

JEFF. But you're in a tough town! To paraphrase an old Polish saying — It's better to be rich and dead than to be poor and living in New York. Do brah nitz. Tomorrow morning I give this to Mr. Prince.

JOHN. Gee, thanks, Mr. Golumpki.
JEFF. Have a good night now.

(*JEFF exits "1" and JOHN sings.*)

ALTERNATE BALLADE

BOY FROM TENNESSEE

I WAS A BOY IN TENNESSEE
MY DADDY AND ME WE COULD NEVER AGREE
HE DID HIMSELF IN HIS HOME MADE WINE
TRYING TO DEAL WITH WORKING NIGHTS IN
   THE MINE
HE JUST SEEMED TO BE A HANGER ON
AN AUTUMN TREE WITH ALL ITS COLOR GONE
I NEVER KNEW HOW HE DID LIVE
GIVING THE MINE ALL THE THINGS HE HAD
   TO GIVE

NO, I'M GONNA FIND THE HOPE AND THE LAUGHTER
A TASTE OF LIFE IS WHAT I'M AFTER
GONNA REACH OUT FOR MY IDEAL
REACH OUT FOR THE JOY THAT EVERY MAN
   SHOULD FEEL

I WENT TO N.Y. TO MAKE HISTORY
I THOUGHT AN ACTOR'S LIFE WAS THE LIFE
   FOR ME
I TOLD MYSELF THERE WAS CERTAIN TO BE
ANOTHER ROLE – SOMETHING ELSE FOR ME
I WASN'T MEANT TO BURY MY SOUL DOWN IN
   THE MINE
DIGGIN' SOMEONE ELSE'S COAL
NIGHT AFTER NIGHT DADDY SAT THERE
ALONE WITH HIS WINE AND THE MOON
NOW THIS BOY FROM TENNESSEE
HAS LEARNED HOW CRUEL THE CITY CAN BE
EIGHT YEARS WORKING AND I TOTALLED IT UP
I'VE TRADED HOME MADE WINE FOR A BITTER CUP

LIVING IN A HOLE – GOT HARDLY A FRIEND
WORKING ODD JOBS CAUSE I CAN'T BREAK IN
AND NO ONE HERE HAS HEARD OF MY NAME
I FOUND OUT THAT IN N.Y. IT IS JUST THE
  SAME AS TENNESSEE

NIGHT AFTER NIGHT I SIT HERE
THE SMOKE OF MY PIPE FILLS MY ROOM
THERE'S ONLY A SMALL BASEMENT WINDOW
SOMEHOW I CAN'T SEE THE MOON

NO, I'M GONNA FIND THE HOPE AND THE LAUGHTER
A TASTE OF LIFE IS WHAT I'M AFTER
GONNA REACH OUR FOR MY IDEAL
REACH OUT FOR THE JOY THAT EVERY MAN
  SHOULD FEEL

PROPERTY LIST

AVANT GARDE PLAYWRIGHTING KIT
kit with:
   box of cockroaches
   drug dilated pupils
   cocaine
   rat
   Samuel Beckett album
dark glasses
gypsy headband
check
shovel
army cap
feather duster
LATIN AMERICAN TOUR
clipboard with pencil and pad
4 portfolios
2 bald heads
2 signs:
   "Iguanas Saltarinas"
   "Arfo"
1 dog mask
1 newspaper with crossword puzzle
1 trade paper
AGENT
Desk with papers
2 chairs
6 button phone
resume
portfolio with gun with blanks
COMPOSER/TANGO
steno pad and pencil
character glasses (2)
HUNS
clipboard with pencil
rubber ear
INTERMISSION
2 Scrambled Feet programs

CHRIST
bagel
resume
music
clipboard and pencil
GOOD CONNECTIONS
2 straw hats
2 canes
THEATRICAL OLYMPICS
2 Dracula fangs
1 cross
1 gong
THEATRE PARTY LADIES
3 purses with cellophane
3 tickets
1 Schraft's bill
GURU
1 small Hindi applause sign
CRITIC PARTY DOLL
magazine
dark glasses
gypsy headband
critic party doll
kit with:
    bomb
    pan
    large screw
STANISLAW
pushbroom
rose
NO SMALL ROLES
spear
helmet
glasses
CHILD STAR
Teddy Bear
SHAM DANCING
2 flashlights
2 pair tap shoes
4 whoopee cushions
ELIZABETHAN DINNER THEATRE
1 menu

1 cart
1 tray wth dome on cart with "Bacon"
1 joint
1 lighter
HAVE YOU EVER BEEN ON STAGE . . .
duck
ADVICE TO PRODUCERS
2 sets of signs as in script
ONE HAPPY FAMILY
1 "Do an Encore" sign
CURTAIN CALL
1 large Hindi applause sign
SET PIECES
2 chairs
1 stool
1 baby grand piano
1 piano bench large enough to seat four people and high enough
  to be seen over piano.

COSTUME PLOT

The costumes for SCRAMBLED FEET are composed of basic outfits to which pieces are added and subtracted.

ACT ONE

Basics

JOHN — sports shirt, slacks, vest, socks, shoes, belt

JEFF — sports shirt, slacks, V-neck sweater, socks, shoes, belt

ROGER — sports shirt, slacks, sports jacket, socks, shoes, belt

EVVIE — tank top, crepe blouse, skirt, jacket, hose, shoes, belt

Haven't We Met . . .

Basics

Avant Garde Playwriting Kit

JEFF — army cap

ROGER — gypsy headband and dark glasses

Latin American Tour/Making the Rounds

JEFF — bald pate

ROGER — bald pate

JOHN — dog's head

EVVIE — wig

Agent

JEFF — sunglasses

Composer/Hung-up Tango

EVVIE — remove blouse and jacket, add glasses

ROGER — remove sports jacket, add vest and glasses

Huns/British

EVVIE — remove glasses, add armor and helmet

JEFF — add Huns jacket and hat

JOHN — add Huns robe and hat

Intermission/Could Have Been

JOHN — remove Huns, add sports jacket without vest

EVVIE — remove Huns, add shawl

Christ & Pontius Pilate

JOHN — remove sports jacket, add Pilate tabard

JEFF — add Christ tabard

ROGER — add tabard

Theatrical Olympics

EVVIE — skirt, jacket, tank top, shoes, hose, belt

JEFF — V-neck sweater, no shirt, slacks, shoes, socks, belt

JOHN and ROGER — basics for Carol Channing

JOHN — add black ascot for Rebobo
JOHN — add ratty cape and teeth for Dracula
ROGER — add beautiful cape and teeth for Dracula
ROGER and JOHN — basics for Wrestling
ROGER — velvet jacket and beret for Jacques
Theatre Party Ladies
EVVIE — add hat
JOHN — dress, fur, pearls, feathered hat, purse (his own socks
    and shoes)
JEFF — dress, hat, purse, glasses (his own socks and shoes)
ROGER — dress, pin, padding, purse, hat (his own socks and
    shoes)

ACT TWO
Basics
EVVIE — black silk pants, tunic, vest, hose, shoes
JOHN — tux pants, white shirt, sweater vest, socks, shoes
JEFF — tux pants, white shirt, Act 1 sweater, socks, shoes
ROGER — tux pants, white shirt, V-neck sweater, socks, shoes,
    Act 1 jacket
Guru
JEFF — add robe and turban
Critic Party Doll, Love in the Wings
All basics
Stanislaw/Only one Dance
JOHN — change vest for V-neck sweater
ROGER — basic
JEFF — add old cardigan, glasses, cap
No Small Roles
JOHN — add Roman armor, helmet, spear
Child star
EVVIE — "little girl" costume, rock star costume
ROGER, JOHN, JEFF — typical rock group clothes
Sham Dancing
JOHN — substitute dance pants for tux pants, just socks
ROGER — remove jacket
JEFF — tights and top
EVVIE — dance skirt and leotard
Elizabethan Dinner Theatre
EVVIE — intro in dance clothes, then change to evening gown
    with Elizabethan robe and hat

ROGER — hat
JOHN — full tux with Elizabethan hat and robe over
JEFF — full tux with Elizabethan hat and ruff over
Have You Ever Been On Stage . . .
JOHN — full tux
JEFF — full tux
EVVIE — evening gown with shawl
Advice to Producers
ALL — full evening dress
One Happy Family
JOHN — add raincoat

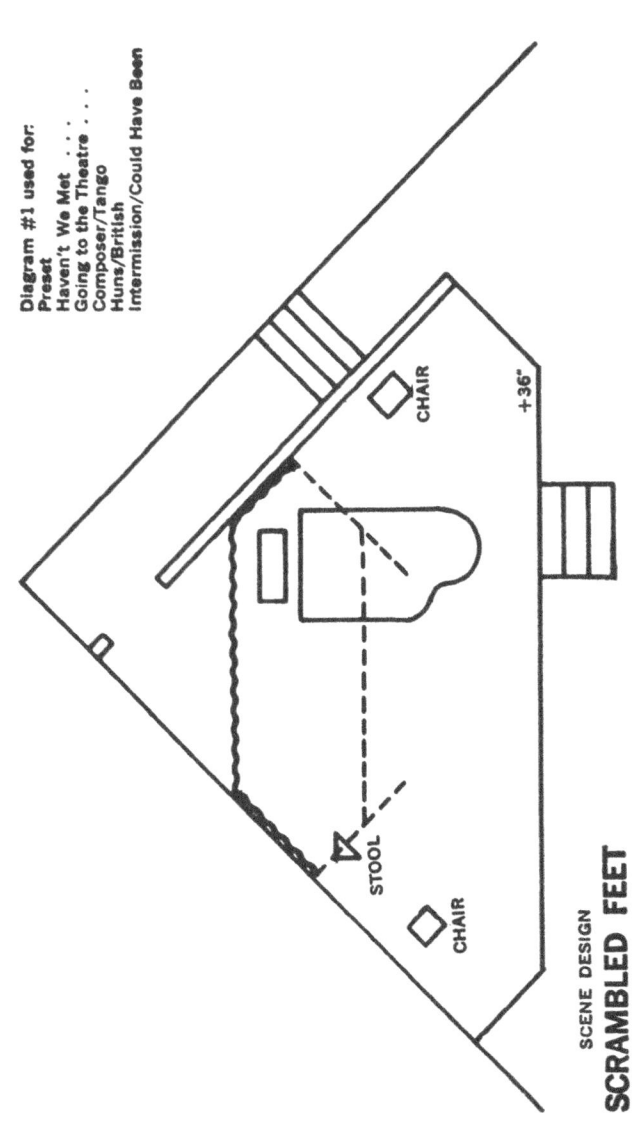

Diagram #1 used for:
Preset
Haven't We Met . . .
Going to the Theatre . . .
Composer/Tango
Huns/British
Intermission/Could Have Been

CHAIR

STOOL

CHAIR

+36"

SCENE DESIGN
SCRAMBLED FEET

65

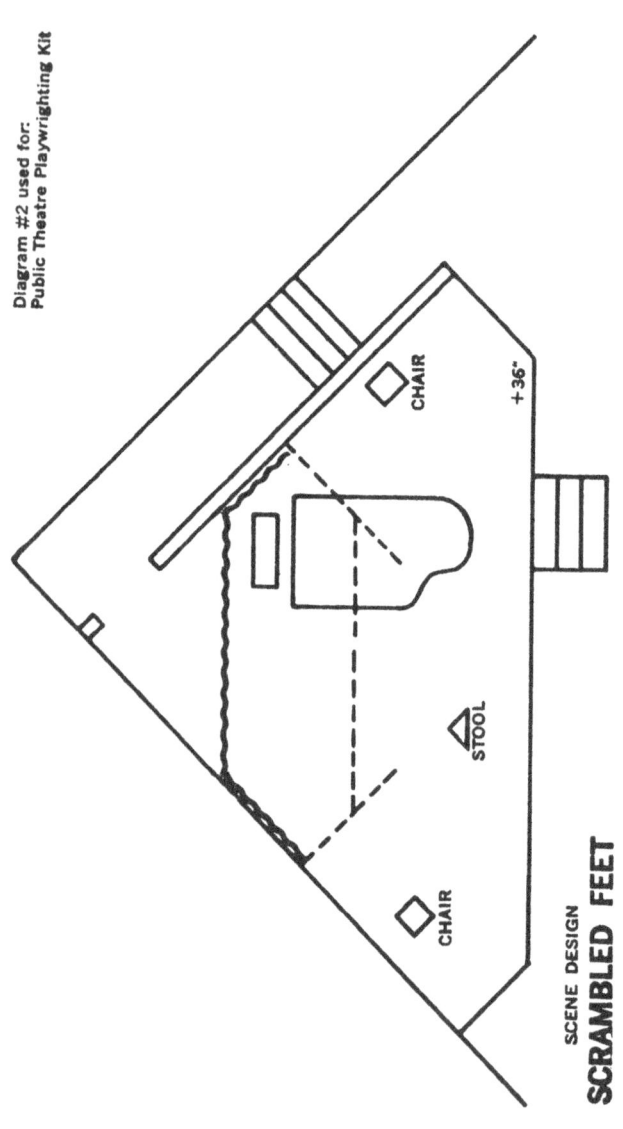

Diagram #2 used for:
Public Theatre Playwrighting Kit

CHAIR

+36"

STOOL

CHAIR

SCENE DESIGN

SCRAMBLED FEET

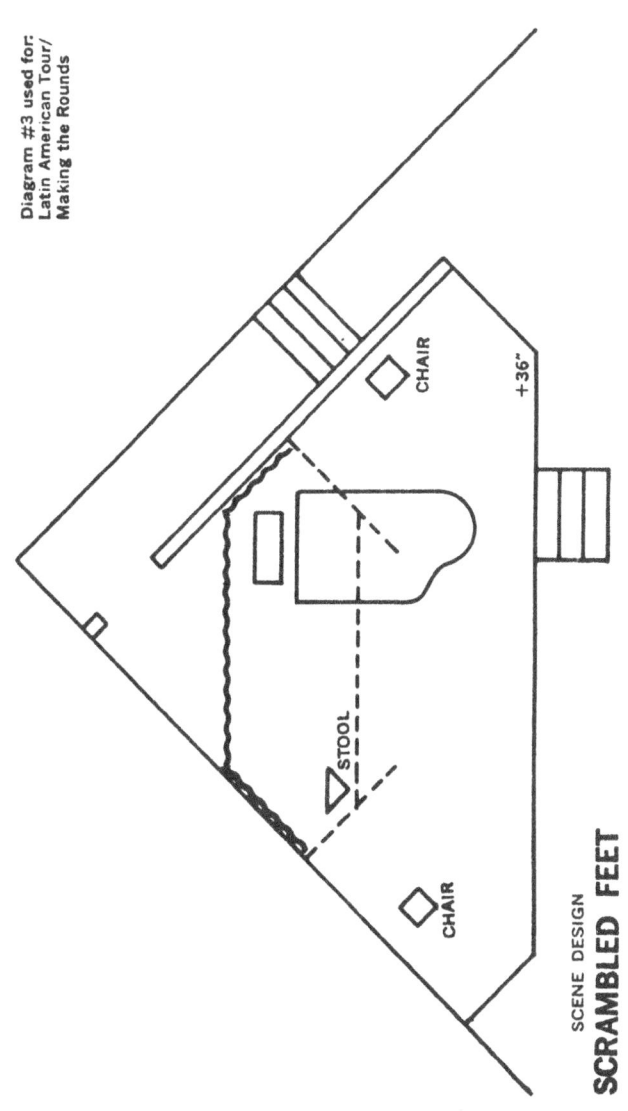

Diagram #3 used for:
Latin American Tour/
Making the Rounds

CHAIR

+36"

STOOL

CHAIR

SCENE DESIGN
SCRAMBLED FEET

67

Diagram #4 used for:
Agent

+36

STOOL

CHAIR

CHAIR

TABLE

SCENE DESIGN
SCRAMBLED FEET

68

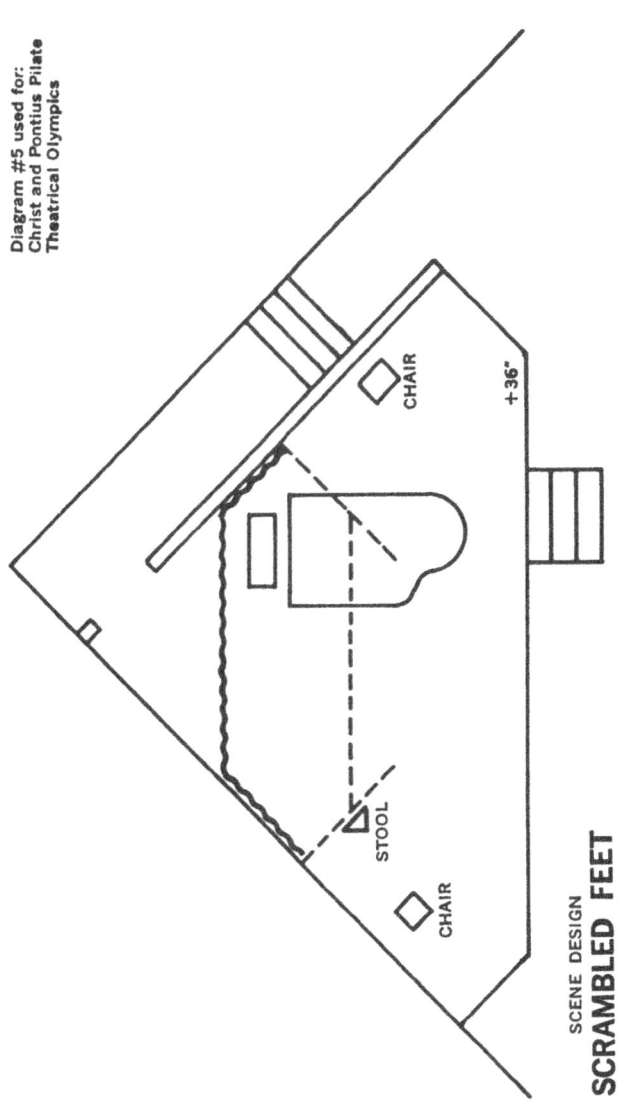

Diagram #5 used for:
Christ and Pontius Pilate
Theatrical Olympics

CHAIR

+36"

STOOL

CHAIR

SCENE DESIGN
SCRAMBLED FEET

69

Diagram #6 used for:
Theatre Party Ladies

+36"

CHAIR
CHAIR
CHAIR

STOOL

SCENE DESIGN
SCRAMBLED FEET

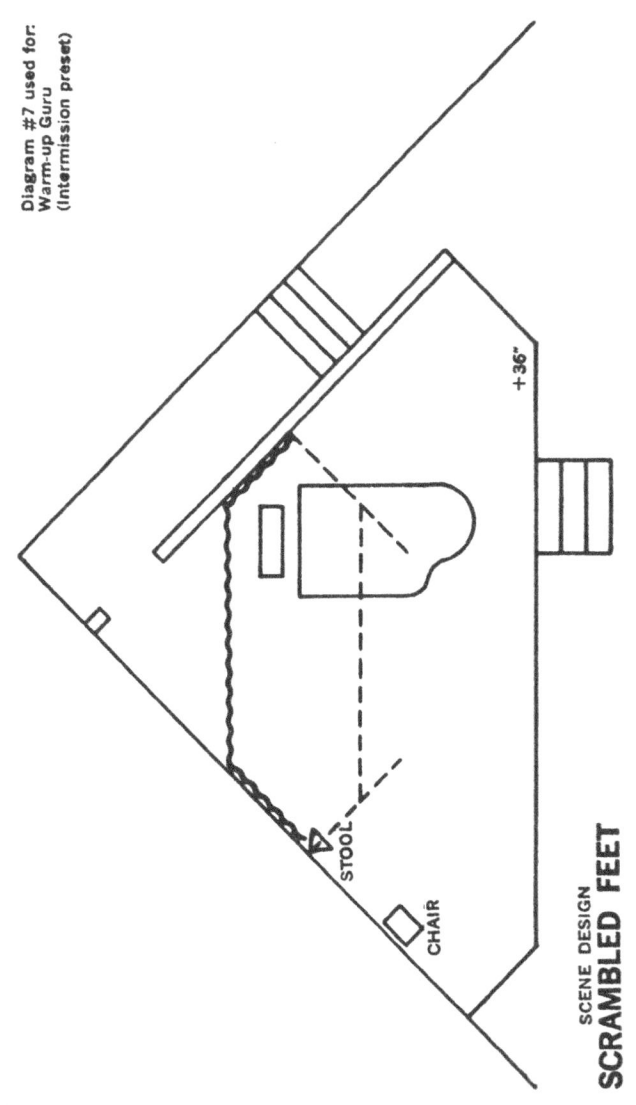

Diagram #7 used for:
Warm-up Guru
(Intermission preset)

STOOL

CHAIR

+36"

SCENE DESIGN
SCRAMBLED FEET

71

Diagram #8 used for:
Critic Party Doll

+36"

STOOL

CHAIR

SCENE DESIGN

SCRAMBLED FEET

72

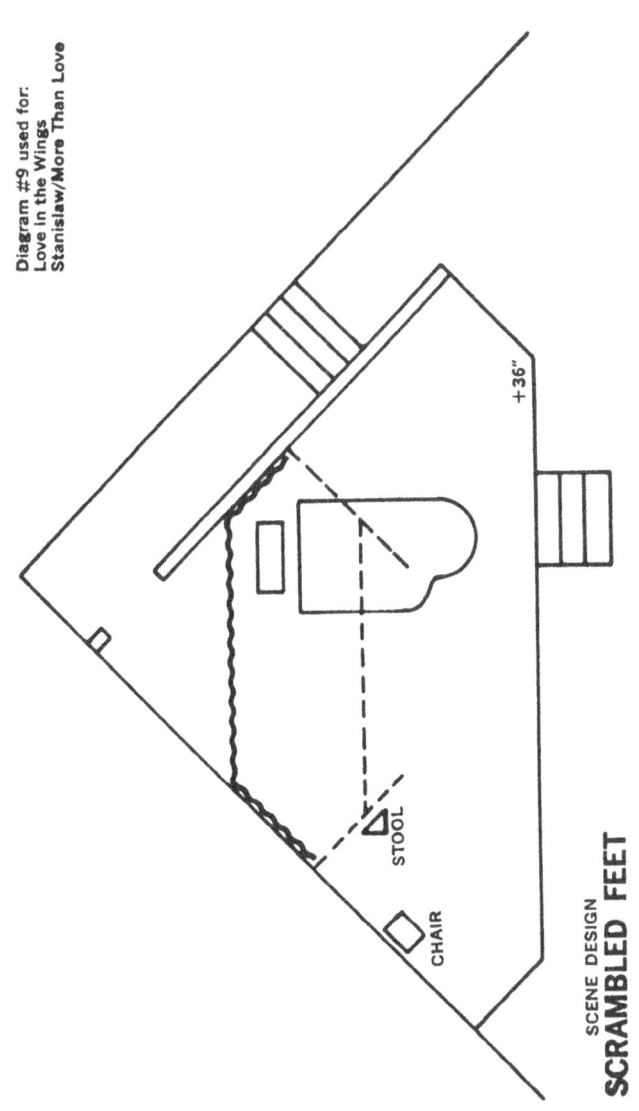

Diagram #9 used for:
Love in the Wings
Stanislaw/More Than Love

+36"

STOOL

CHAIR

SCENE DESIGN
SCRAMBLED FEET

73

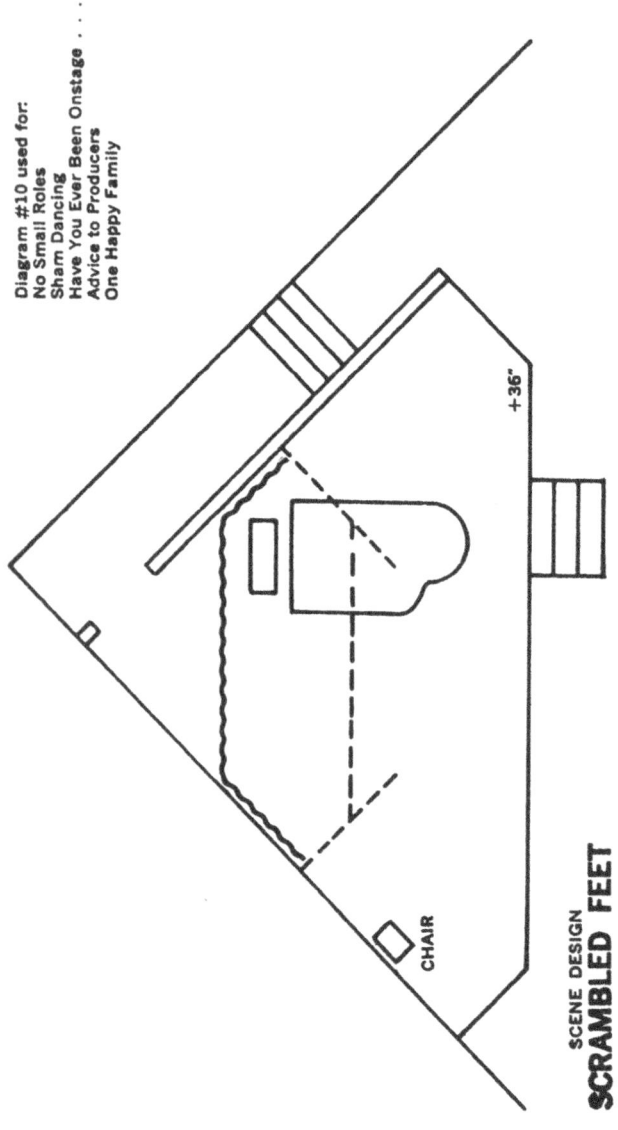

Diagram #10 used for:
No Small Roles
Sham Dancing
Have You Ever Been Onstage . . .
Advice to Producers
One Happy Family

+36"

CHAIR

SCENE DESIGN
SCRAMBLED FEET

74

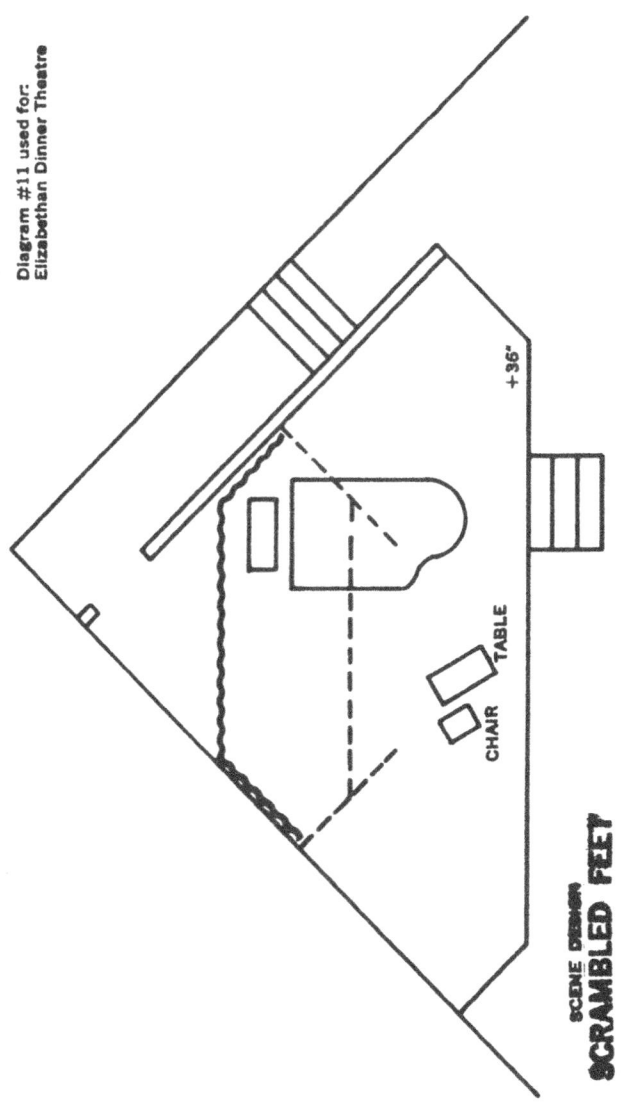

Diagram #11 used for:
Elizabethan Dinner Theatre

+36"

TABLE

CHAIR

SCENE DESIGN
SCRAMBLED FEET

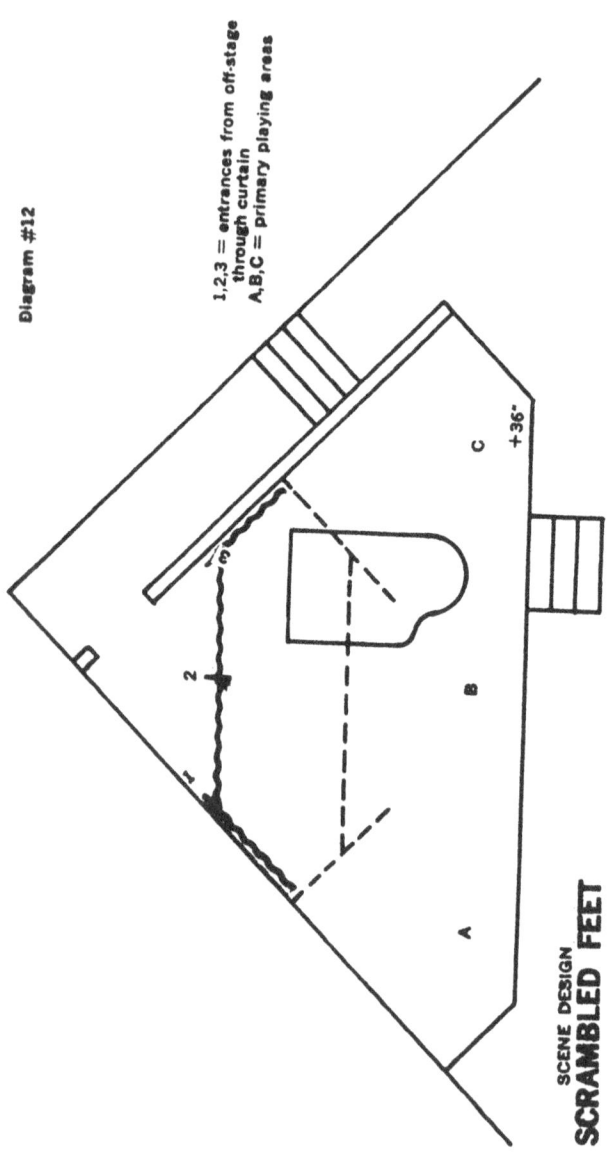

Diagram #12

1,2,3 = entrances from off-stage through curtain
A,B,C = primary playing areas

+36°

C

B

A

2

SCENE DESIGN
SCRAMBLED FEET

MUSIC USE NOTE

IMPORTANT BILLING AND CREDIT REQUIREMENTS